Geronimo Stilton

THE RACE AGAINST TIME

THE THIRD JOURNEY THROUGH TIME

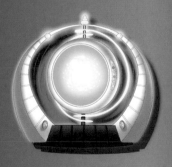

Scholastic Inc.

ISBN 978-0-545-87241-6

Text by Geronimo Stilton
Original title *Viaggio nel Tempo - 3*
Cover by Silvia Bigolin (design) and Christian Aliprandi (color)
Illustrations by Danilo Barozzi and Silvia Bigolin (design), Christian Aliprandi (color), Andrea Denegri, and Piemme's archives. 3-D backgrounds by Davide Turotti.
Graphics by Yuko Egusa, Michela Battaglin, and Marta Lorini

Special thanks to Beth Dunfey
Translated by Julia Heim
Interior design by Becky James

10 9 8 7 6 5 4 3 2 1   16 17 18 19 20

Printed in Malaysia   108

First edition, February 2016

GERONIMO'S TRAVELS THROUGH TIME

This wasn't the first journey through time that my friends and I have been on! My dear friend Professor Paws von Volt sent us on some amazing trips . . .

THE MOUSE MOVER 3000

With the Mouse Mover 3000, the first time machine the professor invented, we went to prehistory, ancient Egypt, and medieval England. Along the way, we saw so many amazing things! Stegosauruses, prehistoric forests, mummies, pharaohs, castles, knights . . . you name it!

THE RODENT RELOCATOR

Then Professor von Volt invented the Rodent Relocator, a more advanced time machine. So we went on another journey! We visited ancient Rome during the time of Julius Caesar, discovered the secrets of the Mayan cities, and danced in the palace of Versailles during the reign of the Sun King!

THE PAW PRO PORTAL

This time, Professor von Volt called us to his top secret laboratory to show us his latest invention: the Paw Pro Portal! Who knew what ancient lands it would take us to? A mouserific new adventure awaited us!

Geronimo Stilton

Hello, dear rodent friends! My name is Stilton, Geronimo Stilton, and I am about to tell you a truly fabumouse **ADVENTURE** story! But first, let me introduce my friends . . .

Thea Stilton

Fit and **fierce**, my sister, Thea, is a special correspondent for *The Rodent's Gazette*, the newspaper I run. She loves traveling and adventure!

Trap Stilton

Trap is a shameless prankster. He really knows how to twist my tail. In fact, his favorite hobby is playing tricks on me! But he is my cousin, and I love him.

Benjamin Stilton

Ah, Benjamin! He is my favorite nephew and a total sweetie pie. He dreams of someday becoming a great journalist, just like his uncle Geronimo.

Bugsy Wugsy

Bugsy Wugsy is Benjamin's best friend, a cheerful and lively little rodent. Sometimes she can be a bit *too* lively, but I must confess she is irresistibly sweet!

Paws von Volt

A genius inventor, Professor von Volt has dedicated his life to scientific experiments of all kinds. He even built a Paw Pro Portal to *travel* through time!

MY NAME IS STILTON, GERONIMO STILTON . . .

Hello there! It's so nice to see you! My name is Stilton, *Geronimo Stilton*. I run *The Rodent's Gazette*, the most famouse newspaper on Mouse Island.

The night it all started, it was late in the evening when I left the office, and I was very **tired**. I was more than tired — I was downright exhausted!

I'm finally home!

I dragged my tail behind me as I crossed through the streets of my beloved New Mouse City.

When I finally reached my cozy little mouse hole, I closed the door and sighed contentedly. I was so happy to be home!

I went to the fridge and pulled out a slice of **Parmesan pie**.

Then I drank a cup of chamomile tea. I brushed my **TEETH**.

I slipped into my favorite **pj's**.

I slid into my **SLIPPERS** and headed for bed.

I finally got under the **covers** . . .

And I fell asleep. It was already ten o'clock!

A moment later, the telephone *rang*. I jumped up.

"Holey cheese, who is calling me at this hour?" I squeaked, alarmed.

GERONIMOOOOO!

"**Geroni-meeeeeoowww!**" a familiar squeak screamed.

I sighed. It was my cousin **Trap**!

"Hello, Trap. Could you please call me by my real name, Geronimo?"

"Sure! Gerrykins, what are you doing? Sleeping?"

"Not anymore," I muttered. "And my name is **G-E-R-O-N-I-M-O**."

He snickered. "Of course it is, Gerry Berry."

I was about to protest, but he cut me off. "I'm calling because I need to see you tomorrow morning at nine o'clock in Singing Stone Plaza. Meet me by the bookstore on the corner."

I yawned. "Okay, see you then. Good night."

I hung up and snuggled into bed again. It was ten thirty, and I was beat!

But then the phone rang again.

Yawning, I answered, "Hello, this is Geronimo . . ."

"Hey, Gerrymouse, it's **me** again! You know, Trap! I wanted to make sure you understood me. It's Singing Stone Plaza, the **square** with the statue in the middle . . . and the bookstore is the one on the CORNER, between the Cheddar Chopper and that whisker-licking-good ICE-CREAM SHOP!"

"I understood you perfectly the first time, Trap," I said. "Would you mind if I go back to sleep?"

I hung up and put my snout back on my pillow.

At midnight, the phone rang again.

Blearily, I answered, "Hello, this is Stil—"

It was Trap. "Cousinkins, I'm calling to **remind** you about our meeting tomorrow morning," he squeaked. "Did you set your alarm? You know, sometimes rodents forget to set the alarm and then they don't wake up in time . . ."

Ring ring riiiing!

"I SET MY ALARM!" I yelled at the top of my lungs.

Enough!

"Ger-Ger, your squeak sounds a little **hoarse!**" He snickered. "Why don't you have some chamomile tea?"

"I already had some chamomile tea! I was **SNOOZING** soundly before you called me!"

I chewed Trap out like a beaver building a dam. But that didn't stop him from calling me **again** at 3:00 a.m.

"Germeister, take this short quiz:

Argh!

1) **WHO** are you meeting tomorrow?

2) WHERE?

3) At what **time**?"

"I'm meeting *you*! In Singing Stone Plaza! At nine!" I **EXPLODED** in exasperation.

"Well done! I didn't take you for such a smartytail!" he replied.

"Please, Trap, can you let me sleep now, *please*? I'm **a mess**!" I cried.

At six, my phone **rang** again. I grabbed the receiver . . . but I was so sleepy that I accidentally hit my snout with it!

Ring . . .
ring . . .
. . . riiiing!

Ouch!

With my ears ringing like a bell, I stuttered, "H-hello, w-who is it?"

My cousin yelped,

"WAKE UUUUUUUP!

It's time to get up if you want to be in Singing Stone Plaza at nine!"

"But the plaza is just a few stops on the bus from here! I don't need that much time," I protested.

"Well, you never know . . . you could **BURN** your whiskers on your breakfast, **SPILL** milk on yourself, and need to change all your clothes!" Trap said. "Or the bus could get a **FLAT** tire, or you could slip on a banana peel and dislocate a paw . . . You never know, especially when it comes to a clumsy mouse like you!"

By now, I was too tired to get angry. "Okay, okay, I'll get up now!"

ONLY YOU CAN HELP ME!

It had been a **TERRIBLE** night, and I was more exhausted than ever!

Why wouldn't my cousin let me sleep? He knew I needed to rest for at least **eight** hours a night! For weeks now, I had been under deadline, chewing the cheese block from both ends! I am a very *busy* mouse, you see.

Somehow I managed to wash up and get dressed without tripping over my own tail.

It was still dark. It was only 7:00 a.m.! There were two more hours before my appointment with Trap, but I was already **WIDE-AWAKE**. So I decided to take a little

SCAMPER THROUGH THE PARK.

It's so nice to watch the city wake up bit by bit.

As I passed my favorite newsstand, I picked up a magazine and decided to treat myself to a delicious breakfast from the **bakery**.

I drank a double cappuccino with grated cheese on top.

Then I sipped a cup of *pear and Parmesan* juice.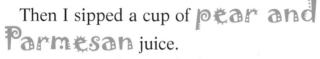

I ate four **chocolates** filled with melted cheese.

Yum, yum, yum!

All of that helped me regain my strength.

I began scurrying to my appointment (it was only **eight thirty!**), wondering, *What's so important that Trap had to keep me up all night?* I reached the corner of Singing Stone Plaza at nine exactly. I am a mouse who prides himself on **punctuality**!

Trap, on the other paw, is not. He hadn't arrived yet.

I began to pace *BACK* and *FORTH*, back and forth, back and forth, back and forth, back and forth, back and forth, back and forth. Each time I reached the corner, I checked the time:

9:05 . . . 9:10 . . . 9:45 . . . 10:00 . . . 9:20 . . . 9:30 . . . 10:15!

I didn't know whether to be *annoyed* or *anxious*!

At ten thirty, my cousin arrived, whistling cheerfully. "Sorry, Ger-bear, I overslept. I was so exhausted from all those *reminders* I had to give you last night! But at least you made it. You probably would've been late if it weren't for me."

I was about to **EXPL⊙DE**. "Trap, how could you? I haven't slept, I've been on my paws since six, I've been waiting for you since nine, and you . . . you . . . **YOU WERE SLEEPING**?!"

He waved me off. "Gerry Berry, you're a bit **anxious**, you know? Stop yammering and listen for a minute. I asked you to come here on very important business. Remember, it's a secret, so you can tell **NO ONE**. Only you can help me!"

At that point, I gave up. You see, my cousin Trap knows my **weaknesses** all too well. When someone asks me for help, I just can't say no!

"**OH, ALL RIGHT.** Tell me what you need me to do!" I sighed.

A TRULY TERRIBLE CONCOCTION

I followed Trap down a dark alley behind Singing Stone Plaza. He lifted the **rickety** gate of an abandoned garage. "Here is my **SECRET LABORATORY**!" he squeaked proudly.

Apparently Trap had gotten it into his snout

that he would become an inventor and scientist, just like our friend **PROFESSOR VON VOLT**!

I tried to squeak, but he cut me off. "Geronimiser, just look at what your cousin has begun! You didn't expect this, did you? I'm gonna be **rich** ... **superrich** ... **the richest**!"

I was a little irritated. The goal of science is not to get rich!

But before I could say a word, he shoved a **MUG** filled with a horrible, stinky solution under my snout.

"Come on, drink it — for the love of science!" he cried. "Someone needs to try my amazing **INVENTION**. I can't sell it like this. What if it made someone sick?"

Now I was madder than a cat with a bad case of fleas. "What? **WHY ME?** Why am I the one who has to be your lab rat? Who knows what

Come on, drink it!

you put in here! What happens if *I* get **sick**?"

But Trap continued to insist. "Don't turn this into a big deal! Just drink it, Gerrykins!"

That's when I lost it. "That's enough! I will tell you one last time:

My name is Geronimo, got it?

GERONIMOOOOOOOO!"

But when I opened my snout to shout, my cousin plugged my nose and poured the stinky solution down my throat. Aaaack! It was **HORRIBLE**!

For a minute, I was too stunned to move. Then I stammered, "And n-now wh-what's going to **HAPPEN** to me?"

"Well, actually . . . I don't know," my cousin admitted. "That's why I had you drink it. It could make your **fur** grow, or give you *green pimples*, or **heal your calluses**. Or maybe it'll cure your craving for cheddar cheese . . ."

"Wait, wait, wait!" I yelled. "You mean to tell me that you **don't know** what effects this concoction will have? Well, at least you **know** what you put in it, right?"

Trap shrugged. "A bit of this, a bit of that . . ."

Now I was really **frustrated**. "So, you

What's going to happen to me?!

don't know what you put in it . . . but you really think you have a future as a scientist?!"

Suddenly, I felt a belch rising from deep in my belly. **BURP!**

My stomach began to **gurgle**, and my snout started to itch . . .

It could make your fur grow . . .

It could give you green pimples . . .

It could heal your calluses!

A SCIENCE
EXPERIMENT . . .
ALMOST!

I ran to look at myself in the mirror. Then I let out a desperate squeak. My snout was covered in green pimples! "Look what you've done with your 'science' experiment!" I protested, scratching furiously. "My snout is bumpier than blue cheese!"

There was only one thing to do. I GOT OUT OF THERE before Trap tried to make me run through a maze or something.

I called a TAXI and went straight to *The Rodent's Gazette*. There I shut myself in my office and told my assistant that I didn't want to see anyone.

My assistant took pity on me. She scurried out

to buy me a cream that slowly but surely made the pimples **disappear**.

I breathed a sigh of relief. Then there was a knock at the door, and my nephew **Benjamin** peeked in. "Uncle G, can I come in?"

"Of course, my dear Benjamin! You can come visit me whenever you want," I replied.

"Trap called me," Benjamin explained. "He said he wanted to apologize to you."

I shook my snout. "This time he's gone too far! He thinks he's a scientist, but he's just a **TROUBLEMAKER**. Look at me! My snout is **greener** than mold on aged cheddar. And it's all because of his **crazy** experiments!"

"You're right. Trap should take some classes

from Professor von Volt. Now, *he* is a good **scientist**," Benjamin said.

"What a great idea, Benjamin," I replied.

I pulled out my cell phone and sent the professor a **TEXT** on his private, **SUPER SECRET** phone line.

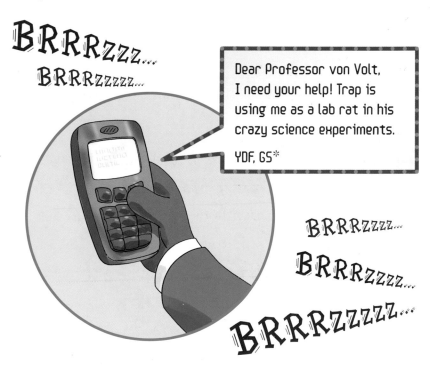

BRRRZZZ...
BRRRZZZZZ...

Dear Professor von Volt,
I need your help! Trap is
using me as a lab rat in his
crazy science experiments.

YDF, GS*

BRRRZZZZ...
BRRRZZZZ...
BRRRZZZZZ...

* Your Dear Friend, Geronimo Stilton

A few minutes later, my phone buzzed.

It was a text from **PROFESSOR VON VOLT**. We planned to meet that evening at the base of **CHEDDAR CRAG**.

The message said:

> Come right away! We'll get Trap lessons from the great masters of the past!

I understood immediately. The professor was ready for a new *JOURNEY THROUGH TIME*. I couldn't wait! What eras would we travel to this time?

Cheddar Crag

is the tallest mountain on Mouse Island. It is in the Nature Reserve Park, just a few miles northeast of New Mouse City.

PROFESSOR VON VOLT'S SECRET

I called Thea and Trap. Benjamin invited his friend **Bugsy Wugsy** to join us, but he warned her not to tell anyone about it. This wasn't like other adventures we went on — it was a **SeCret mission**!

By the time we arrived at the base of the mountain, it was already dark outside.

Professor von Volt!

Sssshhh!

Before us was the entrance to an old **gold** mine. Thea and Bugsy were chatting about Thea's new beaded jeans when I spotted the shadow of my friend **PROFESSOR VON VOLT**. He signaled us to keep our squeaks down.

Quiet as mice, we followed him into the tunnel and boarded an old **MINING** wagon that **ZOOMED DOWN** the tracks into the heart of the mountain. Then we got in a **CRYSTAL** elevator that took us even farther down.

When the elevator opened, we found ourselves in front of a metal door painted **YELLOW**. There was a **RED-AND-WHITE** sign hanging by the door. Below it was a panel filled with strange and **mysterious** instruments.

ACCESS PROHIBITED
ENTRANCE FOR
AUTHORIZED
PERSONNEL ONLY

"And now, friends, please take a moment to appreciate my special **security** system," the professor said. "I am the **ONLY** one who can open the door — the system is trained to recognize me!"

RETINA READER

DNA DETECTOR

PAWPRINT READER

"*PREPARE FOR SCAN,*" a robotic voice said.

The professor put his **EYES** up to a camera that scanned his retinas. Then he placed his **RIGHT** paw on a plate, which scanned his pawprint. Finally, a strange-looking gadget pulled out one of his whiskers, examined it, and identified his **DNA** — that is, the professor's genetic code, which is unique for every living being.

"*RECOGNITION COMPLETE,*" the robotic voice said. "*YOU ARE PAWS VON VOLT! WELCOME BACK, PROFESSOR.*"

There was a whistle and a clank, and then the door slid open, revealing Professor von Volt's **SUPERSECRET** laboratory!

We scampered into the room. The laboratory was full of strange, **buzzing** machinery.

"Professor, what machine will we use to travel through time?" I asked.

"We'll use my latest invention," the professor said **PROUDLY**. "It's over here!"

He led us to a far corner of the laboratory, pushed a button, and a **strange**, round door lifted up from the ground. It was surrounded by two titanium rings, and it was vibrating like a living thing. I put my ear near it, and it let out a very soft buzz: **BZZZZZ!**

Inside there was a weird, TRANSPARENT material, like crystal. I brushed it with my paw. It was as soft and smooth as cream cheese.

"I'm pleased to present to you my new invention," Professor von Volt said solemnly. "This time, you won't need a machine to travel. Just cross through this portal . . . **THE PAW PRO PORTAL!**"

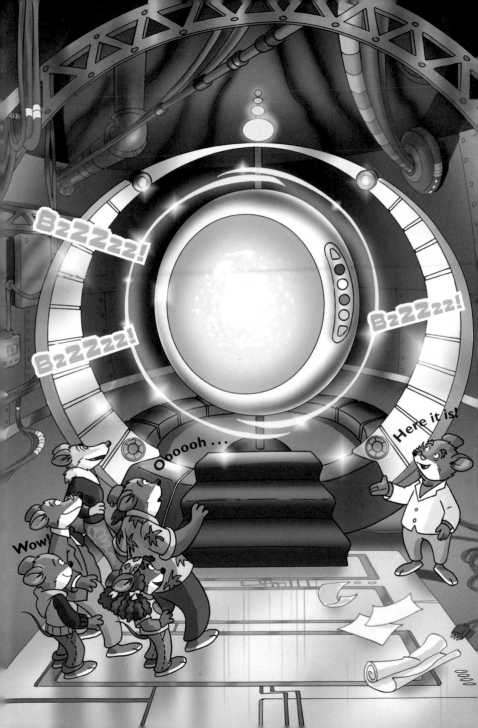

"That's cooler than ice cream!" Benjamin said.

"When we arrive in the past, won't this machine be, a bit, umm . . . **bulky**? How will we hide it?" I asked.

"Good question!" the professor replied. "You won't need to hide it. The portal will blend into the environment you land in. It can camouflage itself, like a chameleon."

"Wow! Tell us HoW it works!" Bugsy said.

"Just a moment. First I'd like to say something to Trap," Professor von Volt said. He looked my cousin **STERNLY** in the eye. "Trap, if you want to become a real **scientist**, you must follow the scientific method, not just try things at random."

Trap looked offended. "I don't do things at random, Professor. I **create**! Plus, it was no big deal. It was just a few *green* pimples on Gerry's snout — he didn't have to make a mountain out of a cheese hill! It was just a little experiment . . . you understand, right?"

Volt said **severely**, "No, Trap, I don't understand. I repeat: A **scientist** must follow the rules of the scientific method! You make a hypothesis, you prove it by doing a series of experiments, you use precise measurements, you check the results, and then you form your conclusions."

"What a load of rotten cheese!" Trap snorted. "I bet Leonardo da Vinci didn't have to put up with a bunch of doubters like you. He just invented **brilliant** things, and everyone thought he was the rat's whiskers!"

The professor raised an eyebrow. "Leonardo da Vinci, you say? Well, why don't you ask him? You'll meet him on your next *JOURNEY THROUGH TIME*!"

THE PAW PRO PORTAL

Professor von Volt pushed a button, and a **BRIGHT** screen lit up behind him. He began to explain how to use his new invention.

"To be able to travel through time, you must open a spatiotemporal **tunnel**. It must be stable, and you must guide it to a very precise era in the past."

...to travel through time...

He cleared his throat. "The Paw Pro Portal functions in three phases:

PHASE ONE   THE PORTAL OPENS

During this phase, two titanium rings rotate to the left at superfast speeds. They create a **tunnel** that leads to the past.

PHASE TWO   THE TUNNEL STABILIZES

During this phase, the two rings rotate to the right at superfast speeds, creating a **MAGNETIC** field that keeps the tunnel stable and prevents it from closing.

PHASE THREE   THE TIME PERIOD IS SELECTED

During this phase, the tunnel reaches a precise *TIME PERIOD*. That's where you come in. You must push one of these four buttons, but be very careful not to make a mistake! Geronimo, jot this down! Ah, I forgot — there will be a very loud 'Bang!'"

THE PAW PRO PORTAL

NAME: THE PAW PRO PORTAL
SPEED: ONE THOUSAND TIMES GREATER THAN THE SPEED OF LIGHT
PASSENGER CAPACITY: THERE IS NO LIMIT!
WEIGHT: SUPERLIGHT TITANIUM

PHASE 1

OPENING THE TIME TUNNEL

During this phase, the two titanium rings rotate to the left and create a tunnel that leads to the past.

PHASE 2

THE TUNNEL STABILIZES

During this phase, the two rings rotate to the right, creating a magnetic field that keeps the tunnel stable and prevents it from closing.

PHASE 3

CHOOSING THE TIME PERIOD

During this phase, the tunnel must reach a precise time period . . .
ORANGE: Ice Age
WHITE: Ancient Greece
BLUE: The Renaissance
YELLOW: New Mouse City
(the present)

Buttons to select time and place

LET THE JOURNEY TO THE PAST BEGIN!

I finished taking notes and put them in my pocket for safekeeping.

"The **orange** button will take you to the Ice Age, the **white** button will take you to ancient Greece, and the **blue** one goes to the Renaissance," the professor continued.

"And the **yellow** one?" I asked.

"That's the most important button: Press it and you will return **home**!" Professor von Volt squeaked.

"That is without a doubt my favorite button," I whispered.

"Oh! I forgot to tell you something important!" Volt pulled a piece of paper out of his pocket.

REMIND GERONIMO THAT THE BUTTONS
ARE VERY DELICATE.
TELL GERONIMO NOT TO PUSH THE BUTTONS TOO
HARD OR TOO MANY TIMES IN A ROW:
THEY COULD BREAK!

What would happen?

"What happens if they break?" I asked, worried.

The professor had a serious look on his snout. "You could end up **prisoners** in time, and you'd never be able to get back home!" He paused and looked us each in the eye. "As you all know, time travel is a **DANGEROUS** endeavor. What do you think, my friends? Do you still want to go?"

Everyone squeaked at the same time:

"YESSSSSSS!"

"OF COURSE!"

"IT'S GOING TO BE GREAT!"

"COME ON, LET'S GET GOING!"

I was the only one who objected. "Well . . . umm . . . actually . . . I-I'm a bit nervous. To tell the truth, I'm completely terrified! Won't it be too **DANGEROUS?** What if the buttons get **STUCK?** What if we all get **trapped in time?**"

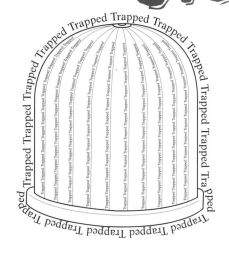

The professor took me aside. "You're right, Geronimo, **TRAVELING THROUGH TIME** is very risky! But think of all the things you can discover . . . of the amazing experiences you'll have . . ."

I sighed. **He was right.** It was going to be an amazing adventure. And what a story to tell! I'd definitely get material to write another **bestseller** out of this trip.

I took a deep breath. "Okay, Professor, you convinced me. I'm ready to embark on this new **_JOURNEY THROUGH TIME_.**"

The professor put a paw on my shoulder. "Thanks, Geronimo, I knew I could count on you! Ah, I almost forgot. Take these earpieces: Each one has a small **microchip** that will help you translate the language in the time and place you're visiting. And now, one last thing before we say good-bye. I've prepared a fresh Swiss cheese

Yum! Cheers! Let's party! How Cool! EPIC!

smoothie for you, and some cookies . . ."

Now I was *excited*. It's not every day you get to *TRAVEL THROUGH TIME*!

What was waiting for us on the other side? What dangers would we face? And how would we survive in the different eras?

I felt my heart pounding in my chest:

BA- BUMP! BA- BUMP! BA- BUUUUMPPP!

We each packed a bag with clothing the professor gave us for the different time periods and slung them over our shoulders. Then I pressed the **orange** button, which would lead us to the time of the mammoths: the Ice Age.

The portal began to **buzz**, and a passage opened in the middle.

I looked at my sister, my cousin, my darling nephew, and Bugsy Wugsy. It was time to go.

We held one another's paws. Then we crossed through the **PAW PRO PORTAL**.

There was a loud **BANG!** and the pathway in the portal closed up.

I felt like I was diving into CLEAR jelly.

In the tunnel, the air was warm and thick, like melted mozzarella . . .

My heart began to beat harder and harder . . .

MY EARS BUZZED . . .

My snout began to spin faster and faster . . .

I began to float weightlessly . . .

Images of past eras and places on Earth I had never seen swirled around me . . .

Then, suddenly, everything stopped. My snout stopped **spinning**. I fell out of the Paw Pro Portal, and an extraordinary landscape appeared before me . . .

THE ICE AGE

DAILY LIFE IN

THE ICE AGE

During the Pleistocene Epoch (2.6 million to 11,700 years ago) the temperature dropped, and the polar ice caps spread across much of North America and Europe. This phenomenon, known as **glaciation**, started the **Ice Age**.

However, in some areas that were sheltered from the ice, **forests** and **pastures** survived. Wild animals and our ancestors, the Neanderthals, lived in these areas.

The Neanderthals were **nomads**, meaning they moved from place to place depending on the season. They often returned to the same area year after year. The Neanderthals **hunted** for their food, and there's reason to believe they **gathered** berries, herbs, and roots to eat.

A little at a time, Neanderthals learned to work with **flint** (a stone they used to make sharp blades), **bones**, and **antlers**. They made instruments to hunt with, like **spears**.

WHAT DID THE NEANDERTHALS EAT?

Some scientists believe Neanderthals were carnivores — that is, they ate only **meat** from the **prey** they hunted. But recently scientists have discovered evidence that they may have eaten plants and roots as well.

PREHISTORIC TIMES

WHERE DID NEANDERTHALS LIVE?

At first, Neanderthals lived in **caves**, and they later built open-air camps. Their **huts** were circular and spacious, with frameworks made of things like wood or the bones of large animals, such as mammoths, tied together, and covered in fur.

The inside space was organized into areas that had different functions: toolmaking, cooking, and resting. In order to cook, Neanderthals needed **fire**, which they'd light by rubbing two sticks together or by striking flint against pyrite, a natural mineral.

MEN'S FASHION

During the last ice age, our ancestors learned to work with the skin and fur of the animals they hunted and to turn them into clothing. The skin was stretched, scraped with flint, and sewn together to make garments and sandals.

THE TRIBAL LEADER

A WARRIOR

A BOY

WOMEN'S FASHION

Neanderthals wore various kinds of necklaces and bracelets made from shells and feathers, and also from the teeth and claws of animals they hunted.

THE HEALER

THE WIFE OF THE LEADER

A GIRL

Icicles on My Whiskers!

As soon as we stepped out of the Paw Pro Portal, it began to **camouflage** itself. In a flash, it looked just like a cave.

We quickly realized how cold it was. The air was frostier than a cheese pop. Obviously, we were in the **ICE AGE**!

All around us, there were huge expanses of snow and **ICE**. I was shivering from the tips of my ears to the tip of my tail. Long **icicles** hung from my whiskers.

With chattering teeth, I squeaked, "Quick, let's put on the clothes Professor von Volt gave us. They'll keep us warm!"

We opened our bags and pulled out the warm, synthetic **FUR COATS** the professor had prepared for us. They really looked **prehistoric**!

The professor had also stuffed them with a substance that gave off a truly primal **stench**. They even included real fleas!

Our clothes had jagged edges and were fastened with **STRINGS** made of fake leather. We slid synthetic **fur** boots onto our paws that tied with long laces.

Argh!

Then I looked around again...

Before us lay an enormouse valley with a stream of clear water at one end. Snowy **MOUNTAINS** stood out on the horizon. It was so quiet, we could hear a cheese slice drop from a mile away!

But suddenly,
the
earth
began
to
TREMBLE!

"**Earthquake!**" I shrieked in terror.

Benjamin shook his snout. "No, Uncle, it's not an earthquake. Something is heading our way!"

"It sounds like animals galloping!" Thea yelled.

"No, it sounds like a lot of **big** animals galloping!" Bugsy yelled.

"No, it sounds like a lot of **HUGE** animals galloping!" Trap yelled.

"No, it sounds like a lot of **ENORMOUSE** animals galloping!" I yelled. "Here they are, they're coming, they're . . . MAMMOTHS!"

"HELP! RUN AWAY, QUICK!"

MAMMOTHS

Mammoths lived on Earth between 2.5 million years ago and 7,500 years ago. These huge animals were herbivores and could be up to fourteen feet tall. They had long, curved tusks and thick fur covering their bodies.

We began to run run run run run run run run run run run run run run run run . . .

But our legs were much, much, muuuuch shorter than the MAMMOTHS' legs. No matter how quickly we scurried away, the mammoths kept getting **closer** and **CLOSER**. Soon they were so close that we could see the reddish fur on their enormouse feet!

My tail was trembling with terror. Any minute now, we were going to get squashed into MOUSE MARMALADE!

We held one another's paws and

MOUSE MARMALADE!

closed our eyes. I was ready for the worst.

SUDDENLY, I realized something. I couldn't let things end this way. I had to try to defend my family!

In one last-ditch effort, I yelled as loud as I could,

"GO AWAY, YOU BEASTS!"

Then something very peculiar happened . . .

The giant MAMMOTH reared up on his back feet and let out a truly thunderous trumpet of terror.

I had scared him!

That enormouse mammoth was SCARED of little old me!

I turned to my friends and said, "Quick, do what I do!" I began to wave my paws around wildly. Then I grabbed two rocks and started to BANG them together.

"SHOO! SHOO! GO BACK HOME!"

The mammoth TURNED AROUND and ran away. The herd followed in his huge footsteps.

I was worried they'd change their minds and chase us again, so we followed them through the frozen meadow until we got to higher ground.

The mammoths were way ahead of us by now — all except one that was limping along. He was very far behind the rest of the herd.

A moment later, we saw him disappear ...

He'd fallen off a cliff! I stuck my snout over the cliff's edge to look. Sadly, the mammoth was lying motionless at the bottom.

It was then that I got my first good look at the bottom of the valley. And that's when I finally saw a stream of smoke rising. A group of HUTS was outlined in the distance.

It was a prehistoric village! We had finally arrived at our destination.

A Neanderthal Welcome

We scampered to the end of the valley as fast as our paws could take us. Then, curiously but cautiously, we approached the village.

At first, we hid behind a bush. We didn't know if the village's inhabitants would be peaceful and friendly or hostile and suspicious.

We observed the **village**. There were only ten or twelve huts total, but there was so much activity! There was someone to tend the FIRE, someone to bring the WOOD, someone to make STONE utensils. Every rodent was busy doing something, even the young and the old.

Suddenly, the wind started blowing our way, and the SMOKE from the fire reached my snout. I felt it tickle, and before I could stop myself, I let out a really loud "**ACHOO!**"

Immediately, all the villagers turned toward us. "There's someone there! Let's go look, quick!" they cried.

"**OH NO!**" I squeaked. "Are they going to attack us?"

Thea rolled her eyes. "Gerry Berry, you're such a scaredy-mouse! Can't you see they don't have any weapons? They're such **nice** mice!"

A rodent approached us with open paws.

"Welcome to our village!"

An old rodent with long white fur placed necklaces made of FEATHERS, BONE, and animal TEETH around our necks. "Please accept these gifts!" she said kindly.

I was moved — and also a bit embarrassed, because we didn't have anything to give them.

But Trap said, "Thank you, friends! We have something for you as well. Go look down there, at the end of the valley! There's a **big surprise** for you!"

The prehistoric mice all scampered off in the direction Trap had indicated. When they saw the mammoth's body, they began to celebrate. Some even started dancing.

The village's leader scurried back to us. "Thank you! It has been so long since we've managed to hunt a mammoth. Without your gift, our village would have gone hungry very soon. We really need food, FUR, and BONES."

Meanwhile, the younger **HUNTERS**, who all seemed to be **HE-MICE** like my friend Bruce Hyena, began to whisper among themselves.

One touched my puny **muscles**. "How could these rodents have hunted a mammoth by themselves?" he muttered. "This one here is so scrawny, his paws are like DRIED TWIGS. Why, he couldn't even lift a club!"

When I heard that, I felt a little down in the snout. I definitely needed to get to the **GYM** more often!

He's so scrawny!

This one's so chubby!

Another one touched Trap's belly with his finger. "This one, on the other paw, is a bit **chubby** . . ."

Trap **SUCKED IN** his stomach. "What do you mean, chubby? This is all muscle, cheesebrain!"

Luckily for us, their leader interrupted. "What are your names, brave hunters?"

"I am . . . **GERONIMOOG STILTONOOG**, and this is Trapoog, Benjamoog, Bugsoog, and Theoog," I replied hastily.

Let's eat!

"Welcome, friends," the leader said. "This evening we will have a **celebration** around the fire!"

"Yes! Let's eat!" Trap rejoiced.

I'm Prehistorically Hungry!

But Trap had rejoiced a bit too soon.

The village leader looked at him severely. "It isn't time to eat yet, silly! First, we must:

1) carry the MAMMOTH to the village;

2) gather the WOOD;

3) light the FIRE;

4) remove the skin, BONES, tufts of hair, and fat (we don't waste anything!);

5) and finally . . . COOK the meat!"

"Holey cheese, from the way you're squeaking, we won't eat till the next ice age!" Trap groaned. "Can I at least get a snack? I'm prehistorically hungry!"

The leader shook his snout. "Trapoog, don't even think about it!"

"I don't want to think, I want to eeeeaaaatttt!" Trap replied. "I'm prehistorically hungry!"

At that moment, a young rodent approached us. She was carrying a tiny mouseling in her paws. "Husband, don't treat these kind rodents this way. Thanks to them, our little ones will be **fed**! Come to our hut — we don't have much, but we will share it with you!"

She LIFTED the leather curtain that served as the hut's door and ushered us in.

"COME IN! OUR HOME IS YOUR HOME!"

Thanks!

Come in!

In the hut, I **LOOKED** around. It was held up by posts made of mammoth bones, and it was covered in mammoth fur. Even the utensils and decorations were made from mammoth bones.

In a corner, there was a pile of mammoth skins the prehistoric rodents used as beds. Clothes made of mammoth fur hung on a support made of mammoth bones. Another **mouseling** was sleeping in a corner, wrapped up in a soft **FUR** that served as a blanket and a crib.

That's why the inhabitants of the village were so happy to have found a mammoth — they used it for **FOOD**, for **utensils**, for **CLOTHES**, and even to build their houses!

On the other side of the tent there were containers made of wood, bark, or bones. Leaning against a **ROCK** were a stone scraper, spears, flint tips, and a stone used to make **SHARP** blades.

With a kind smile, the rodent pawed us

berries gathered from the woods and WOODEN bowls filled with piping-hot broth.

"Here — it's not much, but we are very happy to share what we have with you," she said.

I thanked her. The food was simple but delicious, and it came from the **heart**!

We had just finished our broth when the leader of the tribe thundered, "Stop loafing around

Heave-ho . . .

like cave bears! **EVERYONE GET TO WORK!**"

We immediately left the hut and followed the village rodents to the fallen mammoth. We tied him up with strong *ropes*. Then we all GRaBBeD HoLD at once and began to pull . . .

"HEAVE-HO! HEAVE-HO! HEAVE-HO!"

Suddenly, I felt a piercing pain in my back. A city mouse like me wasn't used to this kind of **HARD WORK**. The rodents left me alone to rest. My back was stiffer than petrified cheese!

Come on! Heave-ho! You okay? Argh!

Massage? No, Thanks!

Many hours later, thanks to everyone's efforts (except mine), the huge mammoth had been **dragged** to the village. Now our hosts could begin preparing dinner.

Meanwhile, I was flat on my back and **stiff** as a rock. "What a terrible start to our journey," I complained. "This is a total cat-astrophe! I've got an awful **backache**, but we're stuck here in the time of no doctors and no medicine!"

HOURS passed, and I began to think I'd been forgotten. Finally, Trap scurried in with a

Ouchie!

female rodent and a very large, muscular mouse.

"Here I am, Cousin! I brought the **healer**, Herboog, and her son Poundoog, the tribe's **massage** specialist!"

The healer PINCHED me on the tail. "Don't worry, my dear mouse, my patients almost always get better!"

"ALMOST?!" I cried, trying not to panic. "What do you mean, *almost*?"

Herboog →

← Poundoog

"Well, every once in a while there's a victim . . ." she murmured.

I chewed my whiskers. I was in trouble!

"I will make you a nice bandage out of rotten mammoth fat and BAT URINE," she continued. "Then my son Poundoog will give you a nice, brisk massage. We'll fix you up! Now, drink."

Before I could squeak a word, she'd plugged my nose and poured a **stinky concoction** down my throat.

As soon as I had swallowed it all, Herboog continued, "Stay calm, my dear mouse! My medicine **cures** everything: toothaches, bad breath, stinky paws, you name it. Ah, I forgot — it also helps you go . . ." She trailed off.

"Go?" I asked, **perplexed**. "Go where?"

But a minute later, I knew where she meant. My stomach began to **GURGLE**. I had to go to the bathroom, stat!

I hid behind a bush and stayed there for a long time. That **MEDICINE** had quite an effect!

As soon as I'd recovered, POUNDOOG came over. "Time for your massage!" he called.

The thought of a **massage** from that enormouse cavemouse was enough to make me forget about my backache! I **scampered** away as quickly as I could. "Massage? No, thanks!" I shouted back.

"Geronimoog is healed!" Poundoog thundered.

"Huzzah! Herboog is a great healer!" everyone cheered.

That's enough! I'm better!

A nice massage!

LIKE A REAL CHEESEBRAIN!

Trap *RAN* to Herboog to ask for her potion recipe. When he returned, he was smirking. "Cousin, when we go back to New Mouse City, I'm going to patent this. I'll make a bundle!"

I was about to give him a piece of my mind, but then Benjamin and Bugsy scurried over and hugged me.

"Yay! You're healed!" cried Benjamin.

"Come and eat, we're all waiting for you!" said Bugsy Wugsy. "The tribe is gathering in the great grotto. That's where they hold all their meetings."

I followed them to an enormouse cave, where the tribe sat around a crackling bonfire. Big pieces of mammoth meat were sizzling over the fire, and a delicious aroma filled the air. Everyone was **happy** because the village would have enough food for winter.

I noticed that Trap was becoming **popular** with the tribe. He was giving out lots of compliments . . . and getting lots of food in return!

"Could you please bring me another **PIECE** of mammoth? You've cooked it so well!" he said. "And I'd **love** another piece of roast!"

I heard two mice near me murmur, "That Trapoog, what a **brilliant** rodent . . ."

"He's so charming!"

"The healer's cousin's sister's mother told me Trapoog knows how to prepare **potions**. Maybe he's a healer!"

"Not like that good-for-nothing Geronimoog. He has no **muscles**, and I don't think he even knows how to talk . . . there he is in that corner, not squeaking a word . . ."

I was so embarrassed, my fur turned **redder** than a tomato! You see, I am a very shy rodent.

Bugsy had heard the whole thing. "How dare you! In our tribe, Geronimoog is famouse and respected!" she yelled.

"Oh yeah? And what does he do that's so useful for your tribe?" one of the cavemice demanded.

Benjamin answered for me, because I was still **blushing** to the roots of my fur. "He tells the most fabumouse stories!"

There was a long silence. Then everyone exclaimed, "OooooooooooooooooooooH!"

Thea winked at me. "In our land, everyone loves listening to my brother's tales."

"It is a great honor for us to welcome a storyteller," the tribe leader said. "I beg you, please tell us a tale! If your story is good, we will tell it to our children, who will tell it to their children . . .

who will tell it to their children . . .

who will tell it to their children . . .

who will tell it to their children . . .

for as long as the sun shines in the sky and the moon glows by night."

I love telling stories! I decided to tell the story of our adventures that day. While I was squeaking, the members of the tribe around me **laughed** and **CRIED**. And a mouse was busily etching and painting PICTURES on the wall of the cave. This was Artoog, the tribe's artist! I was honored to see my STORY depicted alongside all the other splendid drawings he'd created.

I squeaked for hours. Everyone listened to me, rapt. Some were even **holding** their breath. By the end of the evening, Artoog had **DEPICTED** my whole story on the walls of the cave!

PICTURES
THAT TALK

As soon as I'd finished my tale, I approached Artoog and admired his **PAINTINGS**. "Your work is so wonderful! **What do you use to draw?**"

Artoog smiled. "Follow me, foreigner. I will reveal the **secrets** of my art!"

ARTOOG

He took a piece of wood from the fire. Using it as a torch, he led Thea, Trap, Benjamin, Bugsy, and me along a **NARROW** corridor until we reached a small CAVERN. Then Artoog took some dried wood from a **pile** in the corner and lit another fire.

That illuminated the cavern

walls, revealing **marvemouse** pictures of prehistoric life. There were herds of mammoths, deer, and other animals, all painted in **warm colors**.

"This is amazing!" I cried.

Artoog **smiled**. "We don't hunt for the pleasure of the kill, but because our **tribe** needs food. We are grateful to our prey, because they allow us to survive. After capturing the **ANIMALS**, we give them thanks."

He pointed to the **wall**. "When I **PAINT**, I'm also paying tribute to the animals we have caught," he explained. "This is how I express my hope that we will continue to be lucky in the hunt. I learned this

ART from my father's father's father, and one day I will teach it to my children."

Then he pointed to the designs. "This is a MAMMOTH. I drew it big and fat with a lot of **brown fur**. Here, this animal with tall and mighty horns is a deer! And this TALL and **STRONG** one is a cave bear."

Bugsy pointed to an animal with **RED FUR** and long fangs. "What animal is this, Artoog?"

"That is a saber-toothed tiger," said Artoog, SHUDDERING.

Then Artoog showed us the tools he used for his work. For paint, he had wooden bowls filled with colored dust made from

flowers, plants, and ground minerals. For paintbrushes, he used **STICKS** made of bones, wood, and tufts of hair or fur.

"Foreigners, I would like to thank you for the **help** you've given my tribe. I will **CHISEL** your images in stone!" Artoog said.

"Thank you, Artoog!" I said, blushing. "That is so kind. We would love it."

"Good. Now make yourselves **comfortable**, because it will take a while," Artoog said.

"Umm, how long? We don't have too much time," Thea said.

"Don't get your tails in a twist, dear visitors! I am an artist, and you must not rush me," said Artoog. "Now stand still and **smile**!"

He began using a piece of flint to chisel the stone. Whenever we lowered the corners of our mouths to rest, he scolded us. "smile, please!"

Artoog chiseled all night long. By dawn, it felt like my smile was **CHISELED** onto my snout!

At last, he turned to us and said, "Okay, done! What do you think?"

Curious, I scurried over to the mini statues he had made. "They LOOK like us!" I said. But I could barely squeak. After smiling all night, our ridicumouse smiles were pasted onto our snouts!

Grrrrrrrrr . . .

Artoog brought us to another small cavern nearby. A rhythmic noise was coming from it: **TOCK TOCK! TOCK TOCK!**

When we peeked in, we saw a short, round rodent chipping at a stone with a chisel to make it POINTY.

Artoog slapped him on the tail so hard, I was surprised he didn't TOPPLE over. "How's it going, Cousin Scalpoog? It's been an ice age since I've seen you!"

The other returned his greeting with a hug that would have **CRUSHED** an ox. "Cousin Artoog, welcome to my cavern!" he thundered.

Scalpoog was the tribe's artisan. "I am making an arrowhead," he explained to us. "Then I'll

wedge it into a wooden stick and tie it with a mammoth tendon. And these are harpoons made from **BONE** and spear heads."

Next Scalpoog pointed to dozens of tiny flint tips. "We light the fire by striking a piece of **FLINT** against pyrite."

Artoog interrupted him. "Hey, rodents, do you hear a **grumble**?"

I looked around in confusion. "Ummm . . . no, I didn't hear anything."

Ummm . . .

"It was probably just my stomach," Trap said. "Have I mentioned **I'm prehistorically hungry**?"

Now Artoog looked worried. "Can't anyone hear that? Are your ears stuffed with **mammoth fat**?"

I strained my ears, but I didn't hear anything.

Scalpoog stroked his whiskers nervously. "Massive mammoth tusks, Cousin Artoog! I really hope it's not *WHAT* I think it is . . ."

"Unfortunately, I think it's exactly *WHAT* you think it is . . ." Artoog replied.

It was then that I finally heard the strange noise Artoog and Scalpoog were squeaking about. It did sound like a grumble. Actually, it was more like a **roar**! It was coming from a **dark**, **distant** corner of the cavern.

A **COLD SWEAT** formed on my fur. But I didn't want Benjamin and Bugsy to see that I was scared, so I stuttered, "D-don't w-worry, mouselings! I'll protect you!"

"It's okay, Uncle G, dinosaurs are already extinct in this era," Bugsy assured me.

"Thank goodmouse!" I sighed in relief.

"That's true, Bugsy, but remember, there were still **cute** little animals like the *Ursus spelaeus* in the Pleistocene Epoch," Benjamin pointed out. "That's a **CAVE BEAR**," he explained to me.

Bugsy nodded. "And, of course, there was the saber-toothed tiger!"

Now my **WHISKERS** were wavering with fright. "Were they herbivores or carnivores?"

"They are both carnivores, Uncle Geronimo!" said Benjamin.

Suddenly, a **DARK SHADOW** appeared on the wall, backlit by the fire. It was an enormouse bear! He was up on his hind legs, ready to strike!

We were paralyzed with panic. No one dared squeak a sound.

Naturally, it was Thea who saved us. (My sister always thinks on her paws!) As quick as a wink, she grabbed a torch from the fire and waved it in front of the bear's snout, shouting, **"GO ON! GET OUT OF HERE! SCRAM!"**

Then she turned to us. "If you want to save your fur, do as I do!"

My TEETH were chattering in fright, but Benjamin and Bugsy were hiding behind me. I had to protect them. So I gathered my courage, grabbed a burning STICK, and

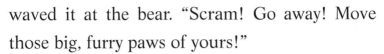

waved it at the bear. "Scram! Go away! Move those big, furry paws of yours!"

The bear **ROARED**, but he didn't attack — he was scared of the fire.

Unfortunately, our TORCHES were burning low. In a few more moments, we'd be bear bait!

But *SUDDENLY*, something very strange happened. The bear lifted his snout in the air and sniffed. He sniffed a second time, and then a third. Then he *RAN* away with his tail between his legs! *HE SEEMED SCARED . . . BUT WHY?*

A SNOUT-FIRST DIVE THROUGH SPACE AND TIME

Thinking we were safe, we lowered our *TORCHES*.

"Phew, that was lucky!" Artoog sighed. Then he pricked up his ears again. "Uh-oh . . ."

Scalpoog **LISTENED** for a moment, and then his snout turned whiter than the frozen tundra. Suddenly, he shrieked and started twirling his club. "Oh no! That's why **HE** left . . . now **SHE'S** coming!"

GRRRRR!

"Who's **SHE**?" my friends and I demanded.

Before Artoog and Scalpoog could answer, another **THREATENING SHADOW** appeared on the wall. A moment later, an enormouse beast with reddish **FUR** and long fangs leaped at us, ready to attack . . .

IT WAS A SABER-TOOTHED TIGER!

"It's okay, I have a plan!" Thea shouted. "LISTEN CAREFULLY. We all have to do the right thing at the right moment, or we're done for! But most of all I need Artoog and Scalpoog's **help** . . ."

"Just tell us what to do!" Artoog cried. "You *saved* our tribe from starvation. Now let us save you from the tiger!"

"Thank you, friends!" Thea said. "I will need you to stomp up a cloud of dust right into the tiger's EYES. That will give us time to escape!"

The whole time Thea was squeaking, she waved her TORCH in front of the tiger's snout. Then she turned to us and whispered, "And we need to reach the Paw Pro Portal. Geronimo will **PRESS** the right button for us to travel to ancient Greece, and then we'll **JUMP** in. When the portal bangs shut behind us, it'll scare the tiger away!"

THEA'S PLAN

1 Artoog and Scalpoog will stir up dust into the tiger's eyes. That will give us time to escape.

2 We'll run outside, and the tiger will chase us. Then Artoog and Scalpoog can escape!

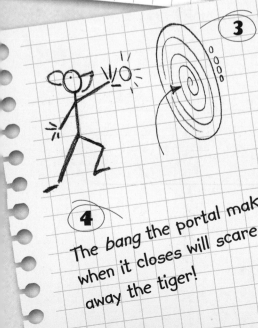

3 Geronimo will press the right button for ancient Greece, and we'll jump into the portal.

4 The bang the portal makes when it closes will scare away the tiger!

"Do you all understand what you need to do?" Thea asked.

We all nodded.

"Okay, on the count of three," Thea said. "**One . . . two . . . three!**"

On three, Artoog and Scalpoog started kicking up **dust** from the ground. Soon it formed a big cloud that made the **TIGER'S** eyes water.

For a moment, the beast hesitated. We took advantage of her confusion and **RACED** outside.

GRRRRRR!

The bright light of day blinded us, but we powered through and scampered as quickly as we could toward the **PAW PRO PORTAL**!

There it was, just where we'd left it!

We reached it, breathless, and I pressed a button . . . but the portal didn't open!

Panting, I realized that I'd made a mistake. I'd pressed the **orange** button, the one that leads to the time of the mammoths — but we were already here!

I tried to adjust my glasses so I could find the **right button**. But they fell to the ground, and I couldn't see anything!

Meanwhile, my friends were yelling in fright:

"GERONIMO! OPEN THE DOOR! QUICK!"

I felt around on the ground till I found my glasses, but they were covered in mud. I couldn't even see the tip of my own snout!

I WAS DESPERATE. If I didn't press the right button in time, the **TIGER** would devour my friends and me!

I realized I'd have to do without my glasses. I **squinted** and pressed my snout right up to the buttons.

Which one is the right button?

● **Ice Age** — It wasn't that one.
● **Renaissance** — Nope, not that one!
● **New Mouse City** — Not that one, either!

The one I wanted must be the last button: the **white** one!

I pressed it as **hard** as I could. The portal's passageway finally opened, and my friends flung themselves inside.

Out of the corner of my eye, I saw the **SABER-TOOTHED** tiger. She was about to chomp on my tail! I leaped into the portal.

I MADE IT BY A WHISKER!

The portal closed behind me with a tremendous *bang*! Once more I found myself traveling through space and time.

Again, I felt like I was diving into CLEAR jelly!

In the tunnel, the air was warm and thick, like melted mozzarella . . .

My heart began to beat harder and harder . . .

MY EARS BUZZED . . .

My snout began to spin faster and faster . . .

I began to float weightlessly . . .

Images of past eras and places on Earth I had never seen swirled around me . . .

Then, suddenly, everything stopped. My snout stopped **spinning**. I fell out of the Paw Pro Portal, and an extraordinary landscape appeared before me . . .

ANCIENT GREECE

A BIT OF HISTORY . . .

- Around 1900 BCE, a group of Indo-Europeans began settling the Peloponnese — that is, the peninsula where modern-day Greece is located. Known as the **Mycenaeans**, these people formed the first settlements, which were small cities separated by mountains. Though they had similar religions and cultures, the Mycenaean people fought one another to win precious areas of fertile land.

- Around 1600 BCE, the city of **Mycenae** experienced great political and commercial expansion. This was the so-called Mycenaean Period (or, the Bronze Age).

- In 1100 BCE, the area was invaded by another population, the **Dorians**, who caused a long period of crisis known as the Greek dark ages.

CITIES AND COLONIES

After the Dorian conquest, it took about two hundred years for cities to grow and rebuild. That's when the most famous **poleis**, or city-states, like Athens and Sparta, grew in strength and power. Each polis had a strong identity and was associated with a god or goddess, who was seen as a protector.

As the poleis grew, they searched for trading partners in the Mediterranean and the Black Sea, and they established colonies throughout the surrounding areas.

THE PERSIAN WARS

From 492 to 449 BCE, the Greek city-states united to fight a series of wars against the Persians, who wished to extend their empire to the Greek mainland. Against all odds, the Greeks defeated the Persians in famous battles at Marathon (490 BCE), Salamis (480 BCE), and Plataea (479 BCE).

ANCIENT GREECE
FIFTH CENTURY
BCE

THE PELOPONNESIAN WAR

After the victory over the Persians, Athens extended its territory
throughout the Greek peninsula and the Aegean Sea. This soon led to
conflict with Sparta, another powerful Greek city-state. The year 431 BCE
marked the beginning of the long Peloponnesian War. The war ended in
405 BCE after the defeat of Athens.

MACEDONIAN CONQUEST

In 339 BCE, Philip II of Macedonia, in northeast Greece, extended his
power over most of the southern part of the Peloponnese. By 335 BCE, his
son Alexander the Great conquered the rest of the peninsula. By 146 BCE,
Greece had become a Roman province.

DRESSING FASHIONABLY

WOMEN'S WEAR

Women usually wore long tunics, called **chitōns**, that were fastened on their shoulders with brooches and left their arms uncovered. The chitōn was belted at the waist. Women also wore the **peplos** — a tunic with cloth that covered their arms, worn belted.

When it was cold, women wore a **himation**, which was a large rectangle of fabric that could be used as a shawl or cloak. It could also be used as headgear.

Women dyed their clothing by crushing berries or bark, dissolving them in water, and immersing their wool or linen garments in the dye. On their feet they wore open sandals tied with leather laces.

HAIR AND JEWELRY

Women's hair was often decorated with pieces of satin cloth that wrapped around the head. Ancient Greek women loved wearing golden earrings and necklaces of gold and polished stones.

TUNICS FOR ALL OCCASIONS

Ancient Greek men also wore the **chitōn**. Young men and boys often wore a shorter chitōn; grown men used a longer tunic that extended down to their calves. The chitōn was held together by a **pin** on the right shoulder and tied around the waist with a **belt**.

Greek soldiers wore thick, layered **linothoraxes** as armor. These layers of linen glued together could protect them from arrows.

The long tunic was used as a party and ceremony garment, and as winter wear. Men also wore the himation as a cloak. On their feet they wore light **sandals**, but when it rained or was too cold they would wear boots.

ATHENS IN THE
YEAR 434 BCE

As we stepped out of the **PAW PRO PORTAL**, a breathtaking view greeted us. There wasn't a single cloud in the sky. The sun warmed our fur, but my whiskers stung a little from the *CRISP* air.

It was a *splendid* and **windy** spring morning. The sea was rough, the nature was wild, and there were olive trees all around us.

As we put on our ancient Greek clothing, I turned around. The portal was already **changing** to blend with the landscape. It looked like the entrance to an abandoned cottage. We were the only ones who knew the door led someplace very **SPECIAL**! And we were the only ones who could enter.

I looked into the distance. PERCHED above us there was a city. "It's ancient **ATHENS**!" I squeaked.

That's when I heard a strange sound.

Chomp, chomp, chomp!

Who was chewing? It wasn't Benjamin . . . It wasn't Thea . . . It wasn't even Trap, and he's practically always eating something!

I heard it again.

Chomp, chomp, chomp!

Someone pulled at the edge of my tunic.

"Hey, mind your

manners!" I protested. I turned and saw a big **WHITE BILLY GOAT** staring at me threateningly.

"What are you looking at? Haven't you ever seen a mouse before?" I squeaked.

In response, the **GOAT** scratched the ground with his hoof. He **huffed** and **puffed** from his nostrils, **puffed** and **huffed** and **huffed** and **puffed** and **huffed**.

Then he took **CAREFUL AIM** at my tail . . .

Ouchie, that was painful!

Just what I needed to **kick** off our visit to ancient Greece: a **HEAD–BUTT** from an angry goat!

As I stroked my poor tail, I gazed out over the legendary city of Athens. A **LONG**, **LOOOOONG**, **LOOOOOOONNNG** wall surrounded the city.

"Hmm . . . how will we sneak into the city?" I murmured.

"We could **SWIM** from the port," Bugsy Wugsy suggested.

"Bugsy, has the cheese slipped off your cracker?" I cried. "Swim there? I'm in no mood for an **ice-cold** bath. It's only March!"

Bugsy shrugged. "Well, if you prefer, Uncle G,

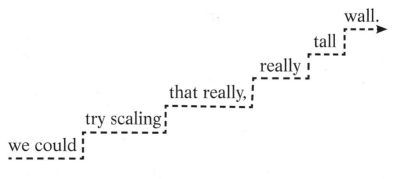

we could
try scaling
that really,
really
tall
wall.

We'll make great **TARGETS** for the guards!"

It was like choosing between moldy mozzarella and slime-encrusted cheddar. What was **Worse**, an ice-water bath or tumbling tail over snout from a hundred-foot wall?

An arrow in my tail seemed slightly worse. So I jumped into the bay. **Aaaack!** The water was **colder** than the ice age we'd just left behind.

And the waves were very, very, very, very, very, very high!

Come on!

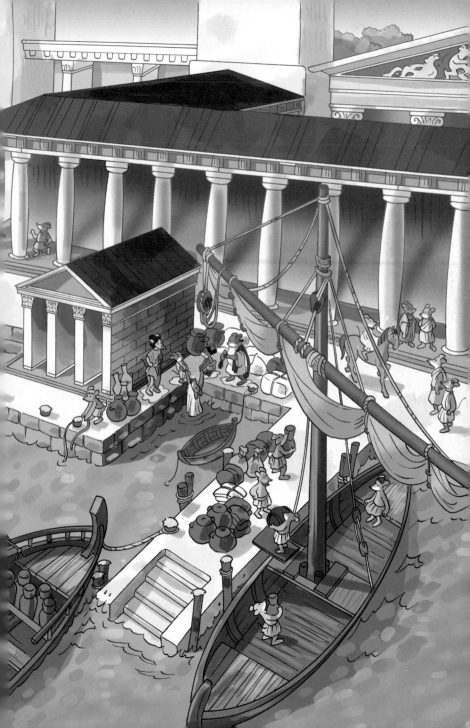

THE PORT OF PIRAEUS

We'd finally made it into Athens, but my fur was **FROZEN STIFF** and my snout was stuffy!

Meanwhile, the port of Athens — the famouse city Piraeus — was bustling with activity. Many rodents laden with goods were **COMING** and **GOING** along the dock.

Fishermice with wrinkly, seaworn snouts unloaded freshly caught **FISH**. On the ship decks, sailors pulled up anchors and hauled sails, 𝒔𝒊𝒏𝒈𝒊𝒏𝒈 happily as they worked.

On another dock, a crowd of rodent families stood with their **belongings**. They were colonists — Greek citizens leaving Athens to live in Greek territories overseas.

THEY WERE SO BRAVE! The places they were going to were uncharted and unknown to the Greeks.

COLONIES

In ancient times, many Greeks would leave their homeland in search of new lands across the sea. The colonies — the areas where these people would settle — soon became independent states.

As for my friends and me, we scurried down a loooooooooooooong street that ran between two very high walls. It led right to the center of Athens!

La, la, la!

Time to go!

Quick!

Hi-ho!

Quack!

Cluck, cluck!

Here we go!

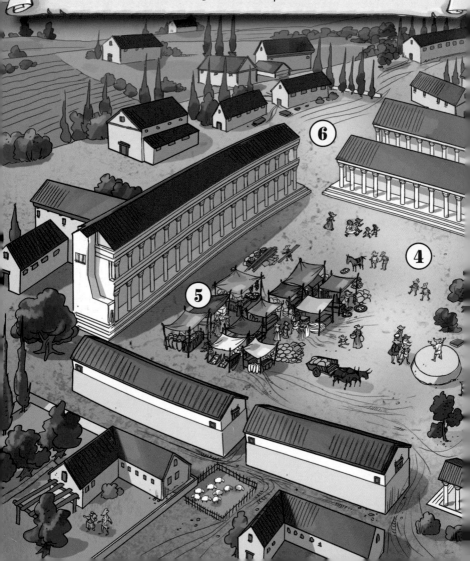

KEY

1. ACROPOLIS: The highest and most fortified area of an ancient Greek city.
2. THOLOS: A circular building. In Athens, it was the dining hall for Athenian senators.
3. BOULEUTERION: The council of citizens would meet here.
4. AGORA: The main open meeting space of the city.
5. Stands in the market.
6. The main street from the city to the acropolis.

STROLLING THE STREETS OF ATHENS

We walked until our paws **curled up** like old cheese curds. I was exhausted.

Around us, many rodents were hurrying toward the center of the city. We scampered with them until finally, at eleven a.m., we reached a large **SQUARE**.

"This is incredible!" I squeaked in excitement. "We are *really* in the **AGORA**! In the cradle of civilization . . ."

"Who cares about cradles?" Trap scoffed. "I'll take a kitchen over a cradle any day. Hey, that reminds me . . . when do we eat?"

"**Trap**, all you ever think about is eating!" I said, sneezing.

We strolled through a marketplace of stands

selling **fabric**, **CATTLE**, **FISH**, vegetables, **OIL**, and beautifully decorated vases.

Ahead of us, in the **SHADE** of a portico, stood a bunch of rodents talking heatedly. In the center of the group was a **small**, older rodent with a **thoughtful** look on his snout. All the other mice were listening to him.

Looking into the eyes of a young rodent, he asked, "Tell me, my dear, **what is . . . virtue?**"

The young rodent thought for a bit. "It is doing GOOD, Master."

"You're right, but then, tell me, what is 'GOOD'?" the first mouse asked.

Socrates

I was so excited. We were standing before the great philosopher and teacher **SOCRATES**!

At that moment, a female rodent with red fur interrupted. "Come on, Socrates, come eat!"

Xanthippe

"Right away, **Xanthippe**," the philosopher replied.

"Come, your soup is getting **cold**!" she called. "You can chat later."

"Actually, we weren't chatting— we were talking about **philosophy**, Xanthippe," the philosopher said. "It's a serious thing."

"Well, all I know is that your soup is getting **cold**," said Xanthippe.

She turned toward us. "Socrates always says he's coming, and then he stays here for **HOURS** and **HOURS** thinking!"

> **PHILOSOPHY**
>
> Philosophy comes from a Greek word meaning "love of wisdom." Philosophy tries to find answers to the greatest questions that humankind asks about the self and the world.

"You are right to call him, ma'am," Trap said. "When soup is **cold**, it doesn't taste right."

"You see, Socrates, this

nice young rodent agrees with me!" Xanthippe said.

"Trap, can't you see you're interrupting a master at work?" I asked my cousin.

Trap grumbled and rubbed his belly. "My stomach is EMPTIER than a candy store the day after Halloween! When do we eat?"

Socrates turned to look at us. "Foreigners, don't mind **Xanthippe**. She badgers me all night and day, but she is a *kind* rodent. And she is also a great COOK!"

"I'll bet her soup is really tasty!" Trap said.

Socrates smiled. "You must come and try some. I can see you are starving!"

My cousin was worse than a hungry cat at feeding time!

Hooray, it's time to eat!

WIPE YOUR PAWS!

By the time we reached **SOCRATES'S** house, it was past noon. We were famished and fatigued.

As we entered, the master greeted us. "Welcome!"

"Wipe your paws before you come in — I don't want **dust** in the house!" Xanthippe shouted.

"**ACHOO!** Please excuse me, ma'am," I tried to apologize. "Allow me to introduce myself, my name is . . . **GERONIMOS STILTONOS**! And these are my friends **TRAPOLOS**, **BUGSORA** . . . **ACHOO!** . . . **THEODORA**, and **BENJAMINOS**. If you like, we will leave at once . . . **ACHOO!**"

"Well, you might as well stay," Xanthippe said, sighing. "Here, take these **OLIVES** and this

THE GREEK HOUSE was a simple dwelling, almost always just two stories high. The rooms were arranged around a central courtyard. Women and slaves spent most of their time at home; free men spent their days doing farm work, sports, and public activities.

barley bread I just baked."

I offered to help her. "May I . . . **ACHOO!** . . . carry the tray . . . **ACHOO!** . . . for you, ma'am?"

"Put your 🐾🐾🐾🐾 down, I can do it myself," Xanthippe said. "Where did you catch that cold?"

I hung my snout in shame. "Down by the port. But thank you so much for the **delicious** food."

She smiled at me. "In Athens, it is rare to find rodents as kind as you. Where are you from?"

"From very far away, where females are **respected** and have the same rights as males . . . **ACHOO!**"

"And that's how it should be," Thea declared.

Xanthippe sat down. "**The same rights?**" she asked curiously. "You mean the females in your country can vote and even participate in **SPORTING EVENTS?**"

"Of course," Thea squeaked. "In fact, I am an **ATHLETE** myself!"

Meanwhile, Socrates was explaining philosophy to Benjamin and Bugsy. "You are never too young to begin asking yourself about the meaning of life. That is what philosophy is all about!"

Socrates wrote in the sand, spelling out the Greek letters of the word **philosophy**, which means "love of wisdom." Then he taught them all the letters of the Greek alphabet: *alpha, beta, gamma . . .*

Αα ALPHA	Ββ BETA	Γγ GAMMA	Δδ DELTA	Εε EPSILON	Ζζ ZETA	Ηη ETA	Θθ THETA
Ωω OMEGA							Ιι IOTA
Ψψ PSI							Κκ KAPPA
Χχ CHI							Λλ LAMBDA
Φφ PHI							Μμ MU
Υυ UPSILON	Ττ TAU	Σσς SIGMA	Ρρ RHO	Ππ PI	Οο OMICRON	Ξξ XI	Νν NU

I'LL GIVE YOU PHILOSOPHY!

Meanwhile, Xanthippe was reflecting on what Thea had said about female rodents' rights. "Oh, how I'd **love** to participate in athletic competitions! I'd become a **DISCUS** champion. I've practiced a lot, actually. I throw plates, you see — sometimes I use Socrates's snout for target practice!"

She tugged at Socrates's ear. "Husband, I just might go off to **SPARTA** to compete!"

"What an *excellent* idea!" Socrates exclaimed. He winked at me. "Then I'll get a little peace. I'll have philosophy to keep me company!"

"Philosophy! I'll give you philosophy!" his wife **complained** as she cleared the table. "If it weren't for me to keep this place in order, you'd spend your whole day in the square chatting with your friends. Those rodents don't lift a paw all day long! All they do is chat, **blah**, **blah**, blah . . . 'What is the meaning of life, what is the meaning of knowledge?' . . . All excuses not to work!"

"It isn't about chatting, it's about philosophy, Xanthippe!" Socrates cried. "Now let me give you a little demonstration. Young Trapolos, tell me, what is it to *know*?"

Trap responded with his mouth full. "Ah, that's easy! I *know* lots of mice. Down at the port there are a lot of **tough** rats who know me. Tell them I sent you and you'll see."

Socrates smiled patiently. "Of course, you know many rodents. And as you say, that's very useful, but it's not real *knowledge*."

"Ah, you mean knowledge with a capital !" Trap snickered. "Well, modestly squeaking, I know a whole lot! I am a **scientist**, you see. As for you, Socrates, what do you know?"

Socrates smiled. "Dear friend, I know only one thing, but it is very important:

I know . . . that I know nothing!"

I was struck by this phrase. I remembered studying it when I was a ratlet back in college. But to hear it from the snout of Socrates himself filled me with **inspiration**!

Lunch was delicious, and the conversation was pleasant.

"Since you'll be our guests for a few days, would you like to come to the theater with us tomorrow?" Xanthippe asked. "There is a competition for the best comedy and the best tragedy. All of Athens will be there!"

I accepted eagerly. I am a big fan of theater!

"And tonight, I hope you'll join me for a banquet at the home of my friend, the great Pericles!"* Socrates said.

THE THEATER

Theatrical performances in ancient Greece began as singing and dancing at religious celebrations dedicated to Dionysus, the god of wine. The Great Dionysia was a festival held every spring, with a competition for the best comedy and the best tragedy. Both women and men could attend.

The main characters in tragedies were kings, queens, and figures from mythology. The plays were about difficult moral choices, passions, and conflicts. They usually had sad endings.

Comedies focused on everyday people and often made fun of politicians and other celebrities.

* Pericles (495–429 BCE) was the first famous Athenian politician.

PHILOI, FRIENDS . . . WELCOME!

A few hours later, we entered a splendid marble palace. A **tall**, **hearty** rodent with a **short**, **curly** beard came to greet us. "*Philoi,** welcome!"

"Um, **THEA** and **Bugsy**, I'm sorry, but you can't come to the banquet," I said. "I know it's not right, but unfortunately only **MALE RODENTS** are invited. That's how it is here in ancient Greece."

Thea and Bugsy reluctantly went to the area of the house reserved for female rodents. Trap, Benjamin, Socrates, and I entered the banquet hall, which was lit by **TORCHES**. A group of musicians was playing in one corner. Rodents lay on couches around the room.

The famous Greek sculptor **Phidias**, the

* *Philoi* means "friends" in Greek.

famous playwright *Sophocles*, and even the historian **Thucydides** were all there!

Since I'm shy, I stood in a corner with Benjamin and listened to the conversation around me.

Trap, on the other paw, never learned the meaning of the word *shy*. He went around chatting with one rodent after another, telling **jokes** and giving advice.

"Pericles, do you know the latest about . . . ?

"Phidias, if you'd like I can be your **model** for a statue. Many mice have commented on my stunning **GREEK PROFILE**!

"Sophocles, you write tragedies, right? If you need advice, ask my cousin. He's an expert!"

Everyone looked at me. I blushed **bright red**!

As I tasted a few **SWEET** figs, I noticed Trap talking with a group of guests. Then he winked at me, as if he'd made a deal.

UH-OH, WHAT WAS TRAP UP TO NOW?

He soon scurried over to me. "I have a **surprise** for you," he whispered. "I've enrolled you in the tragedy competition! And I bet a lot of drachmas — Greek money — that you'll win! Don't let me down, Gerrykins! I don't want to look like a total **cheese puff** in front of all these deep thinkers."

"Whaaaaat?" I shrieked. "You mean I have to **COMPETE** against famouse writers like Sophocles and Euripides?"

He **tUGGeD** at my whiskers. "I know! It's so exciting, isn't it?"

"It's not exciting, it's terrifying!" I yelled.

Trap looked genuinely surprised. "But you're great at writing **TRAGEDIES**! You always **exaggerate** — you turn everything into a **TRAGEDY** . . ."

"But I can't write a tragedy . . . I mean, this is a

THE SYMPOSIUM

The symposium was a banquet during which men met to discuss philosophy and politics and to recite poetry. The diners entertained themselves with wine, singing, dancing, and games.

serious competition!" I protested.

"Excuse me, aren't you a **serious writer**? Come on, get your snout in the game!"

I **yanked** at my whiskers in desperation. "It's one thing to write books, it's another to write tragedies. I've never written a **play** — and I'd have to write it as a poem, too, since that's how they're written in ancient Greece! I don't even know where to start!"

"Well, start like this: *Once upon a time . . .*" Trap suggested.

"No! Only fairy tales start that way!" I cried.

"Gerrymouse, why do you have to make things harder than a block of aged cheddar? You'll figure it out. And don't make me look bad. My name is *Stilton*, too. The family honor is on the line!"

As if I could forget! Trap continued, "Just think — once you're done, you'll be **so happy**!"

"Oh yeah, like that time I kept bonking my **SNOUT** against the wall. As soon as I stopped, I felt much better!"

"You can't refuse now," Trap replied. "I bet a lot of drachmas on you."

"Okay, okay. How much **time** do I have? Two months or so?"

"Umm, eight . . ." Trap whispered.

"Huh? What was that? I can't hear you!"

"I said eight . . ." His squeak trailed off again.

"What was that? Eight what?" I asked.

Eight . . .

"Eight **DaYS**!" Trap whispered. "There's no time to lose!"

I scurried off to find Thea, and explained the whole thing to her. "Even if I managed to **write** a tragedy, who would I get to perform it?"

Thea put her **PAW** on my back. "Calm down, Ger. You, Benjamin, and Trap will act it out. Bugsy and I will worry about the costumes."

"Thanks, Thea. Now I have to go **write** it! Ack!"

I hurried back to Socrates's house and got to work. What choice did I have?

The next week was terrible. I spent every **day**

I WAS TIRED . . .

SO TIRED . . . .

and every night writing!

By week's end, I was so tired that I didn't know what words my paws were scribbling anymore. I invented great passions, gods, MYTHOLOGICAL MONSTERS, **HEROES** who performed extraordinary feats . . .

As I wrote the last word, Trap tUGGeD at my ear. "So, how's it coming with this tragedy?"

I sighed. "I don't know. But I'm calling it **STILTONEIDES** because we are the main characters."

"Gerrykins, I hope you remember I wanted a super-tragedy, not just a semi-tragedy," Trap said.

SO, SO TIRED . . .

"Shut your snout, Trap Stilton!" I cried. "Don't you know what I've done for you? I've been **working my tail to the bone** all week!"

"Oh, Ger Bear, you're just nervous . . ."

"I'm not nervous, I'm just tired!" I cried.

"Uncle G, don't let Trap get to you," Benjamin consoled me. "Besides, there's no time to argue."

"Benjamin's right," Thea put in. "We have only one day and one night to . . .

ONE: Learn the parts,

TWO: Create the costumes,

Think of the fabumouse impression you'll make if you win!

Think of the horrific impression I'll make if I lose!

THREE: Design the sets,

FOUR: Rehearse, rehearse, rehearse!"

"And **FIVE**, run away with our paws up!" Bugsy continued.

"Oh, no, we can't run now. I've got too much fur in the game," said Trap.

"All right, all right, let's get to work!" I said.

Thea and Bugsy started sewing the costumes. And Trap found three tragic **MASKS** and three pairs of really tall, really uncomfortable sandals called cothurnus for us to wear onstage.

Luckily, we didn't need to build any sets, because in the Greek theater the backdrop was **always the same**! So we skipped to number **FOUR** on our to-do list: Rehearsal!

Benjamin, Trap, and I practiced for the rest of the day and all night. But despite our best efforts, **STILTONEIDES** was . . .

A complete and total **CAT-ASTROPHE**!

A TRAGIC COMPETITION

Somehow, we got the show ready in time. Which was good, because the THEATRE OF DIONYSUS was filling up fast.

I was so worried about the terrible impression I was going to make in front of everyone. And I do mean *everyone*. Nearly **ALL** the citizens of Athens had showed up for the contest!

Just then, Trap came up to me. "I have a fabumouse idea," he said. "I just thought of a way we can go out with a bang. It'll be a **BIG HIT**! I will save **STILTONEIDES**, you'll see, Gerrykins! You can thank me later."

Whenever my cousin has a "great idea," I get suspicious. "Um, I'm not sure that's a good plan . . ."

"Listen to me: Picture the final scene, when you play the part of the **GREAT HERO**," Trap said. "I'll lift you up on a rope so you seem to grow taller. It'll be great!"

"WHAT? NO WAY! I'M AFRAID OF HEIGHTS!"

I protested. "And besides, I'm already more nervous than a mouse in a lion's den!"

But the others immediately sided with Trap.

"It's a good idea, Uncle G!" Bugsy said. "SPECIAL EFFECTS can save even mediocre movies. It could work for *Stiltoneides*!"

"If you want, I can do it instead of you," Benjamin offered, slipping his paw into mine.

"No, no, Benjamin, it could be **DANGEROUS**! I don't trust that rope," I answered.

Then there was no more time to talk because it was our turn! We scurried onstage and began to perform **STILTONEIDES**.

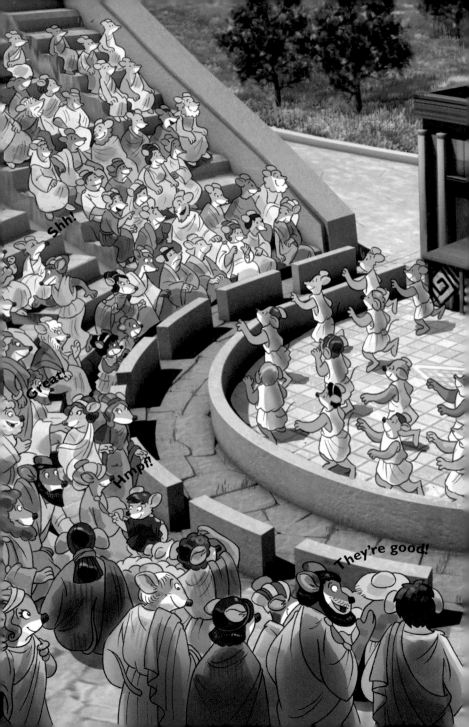

As we recited our lines, I started to feel more confident. *Maybe we're not so bad. No one's booing,* I thought. Then I took a *CLOSER* look, and I realized the whole first row was sleeping. Now *that* was tragic!

At last it was time for the grand finale. Trap tied me to the rope. My snout must have turned as pale as mozzarella, because he began scolding me. "Don't make that face, you're playing the part of a **GREAT HERO**! At least try to look heroic!"

But I was too terrified to pretend to be brave.

"Is this rope secure? Won't it be dangerous?"

At that moment, the rope began to . . .

swing to the right . . . . ➤   ◄ . . . *then swing to the left* . . .

A moment later, I crashed to the floor, completely dazed.

The whole theater fell silent.

Then there was a **ROAR** of applause and **laughter**!

HA, HA, HA!

HA, HA, HA!

HA, HA, HA!

HA, HA, HA!

HA, HA, HA!

HA, HA, HA!

Stiltoneides was a success!

We performed *Stiltoneides* . . .

. . . but everyone fell asleep!

Then Trap tied a rope around me . . .

I swung to the right . . .

I swung to the left . . .

And in the end, I smacked to the ground!

I couldn't believe it. They were applauding! The crowd began chanting my name:

"GERONIMOS STILTONOS!"

Benjamin, Trap, and I grabbed one another's paws and took a **bow**.

Then the rodent who'd organized the tragedy competition (and made the wealthy citizens pay to see it) came to meet us. He was carrying a large trophy.

We had won!

"Congratulations!" he proclaimed. "*Stiltoneides* was voted the best **comedy**."

I was about to protest and tell him that it was a tragedy. "Umm, actually —"

But right at that moment . . .

Thea *elbowed* my right side . . .

Ouchie!

Bugsy **elbowed** me in the tummy . . .

Uhh!

Trap **stepped** on my paw . . .

Cough cough!

. . . and Benjamin pretended to have a **coughing** fit.

I finally took the hint: Maybe it was better to pretend I had meant to write a **comedy** and not a **TRAGEDY**! I quickly bowed and said thank you.

THE CASE OF THE MISSING PEPLOS

The day after the show, we went for a walk in the AGORA with Pericles and Socrates. Trap was in a great mood. He couldn't stop bragging about all the money he'd won in his many **BETS**.

But Pericles was barely listening. He seemed very **worried**.

"Noble Pericles, you have taken us in as your friends. Can we help you?" I asked him.

"Something very **serious** has happened, Geronimos," Pericles responded gravely. "But perhaps you can help. Come, let us go to the **ACROPOLIS**..."

We followed him up the street until suddenly the **PARTHENON** loomed before us. What an amazing sight!

Pericles led us inside the temple, where there was an enormouse statue of Athena that **Phidias** had carved out of gold and IVORY.

At the foot of the statue a priestess was **CRYING**. "Noble Pericles, this evening the goddess's most precious embroidered peplos* was stolen..." she sobbed. "There are only four months left until the feast in honor of Athena. We've been working for over eight months to weave the peplos! There's no time to create another before the **Great Panathenaea**."

Pericles sighed in worry. "Yes, I heard about this **TERRIBLE** crime. My soldiers were supposed to protect the PEPLOS from thieves. If the

PHIDIAS
(ATHENS CIRCA 490–430 BCE)
This Greek sculptor designed all the sculptures in the Parthenon. He is most famous for his statues of Zeus at Olympia and Athena at the Parthenon. He was a great friend of Pericles.

* See page 116. A peplos to decorate the statue of the goddess Athena was prepared for the Great Panathenaea, a festival honoring Athena.

Athenians knew it was stolen, they would **banish** me!"

I tried to CONSOLE him. "Dear friend, we will do our best to find it!"

My friends and I decided to split up the search. Thea and Bugsy went to squeak with the maidens whose task it was to *embroider* the goddess's dress. Trap went down to the docks to see if any **rumors** there could give him a clue. Benjamin went to play in the agora to see if perhaps a little Athenian **mouseling** had noticed something **strange**. And I stayed at the Parthenon to search for CLUES.

We said good-bye and made plans to meet up that evening at Socrates's house.

???

INVESTIGATING A MYSTERY

I decided to examine the locations where the maidens had been embroidering the peplos. But I didn't find **ANY CLUES** there: no pawprints, no forced doors . . .

Strange, very strange!

Hmm . . .

Then I inspected the chest where the goddess Athena's precious peplos had been kept. Hmm . . . no one had **forced** open the chest.

Strange, very strange!

I was about to close it when I felt something sticky on the lid. I licked my paw. It was HONEY!

Strange, very strange!

I looked around and noticed something on the doorjamb a few feet away. Flies were buzzing

Hmm, yum!

around it. There was more HONEY there!

Strange, very strange!

I followed the sweet trail to see where it led.

The traces of HONEY led me outside the temple, along the stairs, and then onto the **dusty** street. A few feet away, the trail ended — it had been wiped away by all the passing rodents. **What a shame!**

Slowly, I began walking toward Socrates's house. I was thinking **and thinking and thinking...**

When I finally made it back, it was **sunset**. Thea, Bugsy, Trap, and Benjamin had already returned. They were sitting in the shade of the arbor, having a lively **discussion**.

"So, did you discover anything?" I asked.

Trap was down in the snout. "I haven't learned a cheese crumb about this case! The **SEWER RATS** at the port were as boring as a meal without cheese. I went to all the most notorious thieves' lairs. Everyone was complaining about the **dry spell** in crime these days! There haven't been any thefts, there's no loot on the loose . . . no one knows **ANYTHING** about **ANYTHING**."

"Thanks, Trap. That's a **CLUE**, too. No one knows anything," I murmured.

Strange, very strange!

Thea and Bugsy hadn't discovered anything, either — no whispering, no gossip. Thea said the maidens were just **worried** about having to do their work all over again.

"I'm sorry, Uncle, I didn't find any clues," Benjamin said. "I played with the 𝕬thenian mouselings all day, but none of them noticed anything odd."

"I didn't uncover any evidence, either, but I did make friends with a *nice* mouseling," Bugsy Wugsy said. "She helped make the goddess's peplos. She was too young to embroider it, but she helped keep the skeins of colored thread in order. She wants to become an embroiderer one day. Her name is Melissa. In Greek, it means **Bee**! And she loves sweets made of honey — she even gave me one!"

That gave me a *brilliant* idea. "Holey cheese! Bugsy, do you know where your friend lives? Let's go talk to her right away."

ALL BECAUSE OF A JAR OF HONEY!

We all scurried off to see Melissa. Half an hour later, we found ourselves on the doorstep of a **SIMPLE** cottage.

We knocked at the door, and Melissa came to open it. She was a cute little mouse, but too shy to look me in the **EYE**.

I took her paw. "It's nice to meet you, Melissa. My name is Geronimos Stiltonos."

When I pulled my paw away, it was all sticky . . . with honey!

"Melissa, do you like honey?" I asked her.

She smiled. "Oh, yes! Very much! We raise bees behind the house."

I put on my sternest squeak. "Melissa, did you steal Athena's peplos?"

She burst into **TEARS**. "I didn't steal it . . . I hid it! You see, I ruined it . . . by accident. I spilled honey on it and it left an **ENORMOUSE** stain!"

Bugsy put her paw around her friend.

"Melissa, you made a mistake, but it's going to be okay. When you're in trouble, you need to ask for help," I said.

"But . . . but . . . I was scared the priestesses would yell and I would never get to become an embroiderer!" Melissa said.

Why did you steal it?

I didn't steal it!

Bugsy took her paw. "But by covering it up, you made an even bigger **mess**."

I nodded. "Bugsy's right. But it's okay. We'll help you fix this, or Pericles will end up in a lot of trouble."

Trap **ran** to tell Pericles what we'd found out.

"Melissa, where did you hide the **PEPLOS**? Maybe we can repair it," Bugsy squeaked.

Melissa took out the peplos, which she'd **hidden** under some hay from the stable. It had an enormouse

YELLOW HONEY STAIN

right in the middle.

"Greasy cat guts, you were right! This is impossible to get out," said Bugsy, sighing.

As Bugsy and Melissa **STARED** at the peplos despondently, Thea squeaked up. "I have an idea!" She rummaged through her bag and pulled out her **beaded** jeans. "Let's use these beads to cover the stain."

Bugsy brightened up. "Okay! But what should we *embroider*?"

"How about an owl?" Melissa suggested. "It's the sacred animal of Athens."

"**GREAT IDEA**, Melissa!" said Thea. "Let's do it."

Thea, Melissa, and Bugsy sat down and got right to work. Benjamin and I wanted to help, so we told **jokes** to keep their spirits up.

"What's the last straw for a tailor?" I asked. "Losing the *thread* of the conversation! Ha, ha, ha!"

The next morning, the embroidery was finished. It was **exquisite**! We put the peplos in a cart and headed to the temple, where **Pericles** and the **priestess** were waiting for us. Pericles had a worried look on his snout.

Melissa was paler than a slice of fresh Swiss. **"I'm sorry. I acted badly, and I ruined everything!"**

Pericles smiled at her. "Melissa, you were wrong, but you recognized your mistake. And so I will forgive you in honor of Athena, goddess of wisdom and protector of our city."

When the **priestess** saw the repairs Thea, Bugsy, and Melissa had made to the peplos, she

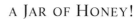

said, "What marvemouse embroidery!"

Melissa smiled, and Thea and Bugsy winked at her. The priestess put a paw on **Melissa's** shoulder. "This is very promising work. One day, you shall become an *embroiderer*."

Melissa was **thrilled**. "Thank you!" she told the priestess. Then she turned to Thea and Bugsy. "And thank you for teaching me that when you're in trouble it's important to ask for help instead of lying!"

Everyone was happy . . . except for Trap.

THE GREEK GODS

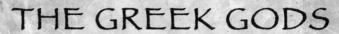

ZEUS

The father of the gods. God of the sky and of lightning.

HERA

Zeus's wife. Protector of marriage.

POSEIDON

Zeus's brother. God of the sea and water.

DEMETER

Zeus's sister. Goddess of the harvest and agriculture.

HESTIA

Zeus's sister. Goddess of the hearth.

ARES

Zeus and Hera's son. The god of war.

APHRODITE

Zeus's daughter. Goddess of love and beauty.

APOLLO

Zeus's son and Artemis's twin. God of music and poetry.

ARTEMIS

Zeus's daughter and Apollo's twin. Goddess of the woods and the hunt.

HEPHAESTUS

Zeus and Hera's son. God of fire, protector of blacksmiths and metals.

HERMES

Zeus's son. Messenger of the gods and protector of travelers.

ATHENA

Zeus's daughter. Goddess of wisdom and war.

A STRATEGIC RETREAT

Trap was wringing his paws, twitching his tail, and his whiskers were dripping with *sweat*.

"Are you okay?" I asked him.

"Umm, you know my bets? Well, I lost everything!" he moaned. "You see, we didn't win the **TRAGEDY** competition, we won the **comedy** competition! Now I owe drachmas all over town. We've got to get out of here!"

I looked at Thea. She shrugged. "We've been here awhile. It's probably time to *MOVE ON*."

So we said an affectionate (but hasty) good-bye to our friends and headed out of the city.

We found the **PAW PRO PORTAL** just as a crowd of rodents sniffed us out. "Trapolos, you owe us big-time! Give us our drachmas!"

In all the turmoil, I forgot what the right button was, and I ended up pressing them all!

"It's the blue button, Uncle G!" Bugsy cried.

I pressed the **blue** button. Then Trap pushed me aside and smacked all the buttons again! Luckily, the portal seemed to be working anyway. There was a **buzz**, and the passage opened. We grabbed one another tightly by the paw, and stepped in.

The portal closed behind us with a loud **BANG**. Once more I found myself traveling through space and time.

And once more, I felt like I was diving into CLEAR jelly!

In the tunnel, the air was warm and thick like melted mozzarella . . .

My heart began to beat harder and harder . . .

MY EARS BUZZED . . .

My snout began to spin faster and faster . . .

I began to float weightlessly . . .

Images of past eras and places on Earth I had never seen swirled around me . . .

Then, suddenly, everything stopped. My snout stopped **spinning**. I fell out of the Paw Pro Portal, and an extraordinary landscape appeared before me . . . It was the city of **Florence**, Italy, during the Renaissance!

ᴛʜᴇ Renaissance

The Renaissance

The Renaissance is a historical period that many scholars
date between the fourteenth and seventeenth centuries.
At the end of the Middle Ages, there was new interest
in classical learning and philosophy that coincided with
scientific discoveries and technological innovation. The
Renaissance is considered the beginning of the modern age.

Art

During the Renaissance, artists tried to
depict man, the world, and nature as
they really were. The greatest painters,
sculptors, and artisans had their own
studios where they taught their crafts
to apprentices. They would accept jobs
from the Church, from noblemen, or
from rich merchants. Many artists who are still famous
today lived during this period: Michelangelo, Leonardo da
Vinci, Raphael, and Titian.

Commerce

During the Renaissance, trade between countries increased,

as did traveling and communication. New lands like the Americas were discovered by Europeans. Corporations were formed in cities: These were powerful associations of artists, artisans, and merchants who established work rules and prices for the products they created. Merchants organized the transport of products between cities and states.

Sciences

In the 1500s, scientists began experiments on long-held theories about the nature of man and the universe. These studies led to great progress in anatomy, astronomy, medicine, and chemistry.

Inventions

The most important invention of the Renaissance was the printing press, which Johannes Gutenberg developed in Germany in the middle of the fifteenth century. Now many copies of books could be printed in a few days, at little cost. This helped spread ideas, progress, and news about all kinds of inventions.

Renaissance Fashion

Merchant

Men

Men's clothing was elaborate and heavily designed. Males wore shirts with billowy sleeves and tunics or vests. The wealthier a man was, the more richly embellished his clothing. Hats were often made of black velvet and decorated with feathers or brooches.

City child

Country child

Carpenter

Women

Women wore long, crinkled skirts below formfitting bodices. The neckline was often square, and the dress sleeves were full and richly decorated. Hairstyles were simple, but hair was accented with veils, ribbons, and strings of pearls. Noblewomen wore rings, bracelets, necklaces, buckles, and medals.

Lady

Young lady

Maid

Seamstress

WATCH OUT FOR THAT BRICK!

As we stumbled out of the **PAW PRO PORTAL**, I heard someone squeaking to us. "What in the name of cheese are you doing in the middle of the street? Oh, *grullo*,* why are you dressed in a toga? Are you going to a costume party?"

I looked around and saw two curious rodents staring at me **strangely**. Fortunately, quick-thinking Trap had an answer ready. "How did you guess? You two are brainier than bookmice! We're on our way to a masquerade."

The two **NOSY** rodents kept staring at us.

Oh, *grullo!*

* In Tuscan, *grullo* means "fool."

"Come on, let's scurry down that alley and change our clothes!" I muttered to my companions. I didn't want to attract any more attention.

I turned and saw that the Paw Pro Portal had already camouflaged itself. It looked like nothing more than a smudge of dirt on the wall.

In a flash, we put on our **Renaissance clothes**. That was much better. Now we looked like respectable merchants searching for a deal!

As we scampered along, I reflected, *At least there aren't* ENORMOUSE MAMMOTHS *or* EPIC TRAGEDIES *to write in the Renaissance! This will be our most relaxing stop yet!*

But just then, I heard a shout:

"Mister, watch out for that brick!"

I looked up just in time to realize I was scampering under a large scaffold. And then **everything went black**!

The brick hit me smack on the snout, sending me to **dreamland**! Not exactly what I had in mind for my relaxing visit to the Renaissance.

BANNNG!

Later on, the others had to tell me what happened, because I slept all day, all night, and all of the next day!

A crowd of rodents gathered around me. "Quick, call the *cerusico*!"*

"Get him something to drink!"

"Noooo! He absolutely cannot drink . . ."

"We need a cold compress!"

"No, we need a HOT compress!"

"No, he needs a BLOODLETTING . . ."

"Poor guy, what a BLOW!"

The cerusico! What a blow!

* *Cerusico* means "surgeon" in Italian.

"WHO IS HE?"

"Well, whoever he is, he has a silly snout . . ."

Two rodents ran out of the house that was under construction. They pushed through the crowd, shouting, "Make way: The noble *Mousato de' Mousati* has sent us to assist the foreigner that got hit by a brick that fell from his palazzo!"*

The two rodents LIFTED me up and carried me, unconscious, inside the palazzo. Then they brought me upstairs and laid me on a tall **canopy** bed. But I just kept sleeping . . . sleeping . . . sleeping . . . sleeping . . . sleeping . . .

* *Palazzo* means "palace" or "large residence" in Italian.

A HUGE BUMP!

When I opened my eyes, I didn't know where I was.

What a snoutache!

The first thing I saw was a **ray of golden light** streaming through heavy velvet curtains. Silhouetted against the light was a **beautiful** young mouse with long fur.

Petunia, is that you?

I was a little confused. "Petunia, is that you?" I asked.

"I'm sorry, sir, I am not Petunia," a sweet squeak answered. "I am Dulcetta de' Mousati. But you must care very much about this damsel — you have said her name so many times in your sleep . . ."

I blushed **red** from the tips of my ears to the tip of my tail. I tried to respond with something that made sense. "Gracious damsel, my name is Stiltonello of Geracia, I mean . . . Mousello of Stiltonimo . . . no, Mousinimo of Stiltonimo . . . no, Mousinimo of Geromella . . . I mean, no . . . excuse me . . . I just can't remember!"

Oops . . .

I feel faint!

With that, I fainted back on the pillow.

What a snoutache!

When I came to again, it was already evening. Next to my bed stood Benjamin, Bugsy, Thea, and Trap. Which was good news for me — now I wouldn't make another bad impression on that **beautiful** young mouse!

"Ouchie, ouchie, ouchie!" I cried, massaging the lump on my snout.

You're all better!

Benjamin hugged me tight, and the others rejoiced.

"IT'S SO GOOD TO SEE YOU ALL!" I said.

"Uncle G, how are you?" asked Bugsy.

"Gerrykins, you frightened us out of our fur!" said Thea.

Trap **tUGGeD** at my ear affectionately. "Cousin, why do you always have to be such a klutz? Couldn't you pretend to be **NORMAL** for once in your life?"

I was too dazed to get mad. "Well, I didn't do it on purpose. Why would I ask for a **BRICK** to hit me square on the snout?"

"Jumping gerbils, don't be a **BORE**, Gerrykins!" Trap said, rolling his eyes. "It could've been much worse. You got lucky!"

"Lucky? I feel like a brick is **BoUnCinG** around inside my head . . . and my tummy is twisting itself into knots . . . and I have

$uch a snoutache!"

"Cousinkins, just think of that beautiful damsel who stayed by your side day and night, putting **damp compresses** on your forehead," Trap said.

Ouchie!

My ears grew hot. You see, I am a very **shy** mouse!

Trap saw that I was blushing red as a **PEPPER**, so he

began to tease me. "Ahh, you saw her, didn't you? You were just pretending to faint, you clever rat!"

At that, I turned **redder** than a cheese rind. "You're wrong, Trap! My heart **BEATS** for another rodent . . ."

Bugsy giggled. "I know who it is . . . I know who it is . . . It's my aunt, Petunia Pretty Paws!"

Fortunately, Thea intervened. "That's enough. Can't you see he's more confused than a cat in a dog kennel? Leave him alone. Let's hurry up — our hosts are waiting for us for lunch."

We headed **DOWN** the big marble stairway and went **DOWN** to the first floor.

A MOMENTOUS MEAL

We were **SO ELEGANT** in our exquisite Renaissance attire. Thea and Bugsy looked like two *gracious damsels*, Benjamin was a very sophisticated young gent, and Trap had the satisfied air of a wealthy merchant.

We hesitated before a wooden door with a sweet tune coming from behind it.

It was the delicate sound of a lute.

A servant bowed and ushered us in. "Please enter, sirs and madams!"

A moment later, we were inside a marvemouse room whose walls were covered

in **FRESCOES**. Other guests were already seated around a long, *lavish* table.

I bowed. "Thank you for your hospitality. We are the *de' Stiltonini* family. My name is Geronimuccio de' Stiltonini. May I present damsels Thea and Bugsina, and Benjamino and Mr. Trapolindo."

Mousato de' Mousati invited me to take a seat. "Please, make yourselves comfortable. You already know my daughter, *Dulcetta*..."

I greeted her with burning ears. "Thank you, young lady, for **curing** me." I tried to bow, but the bump on my head had left me a little dizzy. My snout began to spin. I lost my balance and **TRIPPED** over a chair.

Desperate to stay on my paws, I grabbed the shoulders of a passing servant. Unfortunately, he was holding a tray with an enormouse **BOWL** of cabbage soup!

The tray flew into the air, **spinning** across the room. It landed in the middle of the table, knocking over a bowl of **fruit**!

The soup bowl ended up on top of a female noblemouse's snout . . . and the cabbage soup ended up all over my embroidered coat!

HOLEY CHEESE, WHAT A CAT-ASTROPHE!

My sister, Thea, came to my rescue. "Please excuse my poor brother. The **blow** to his snout

I am honored . . .

I tried to bow, but I got dizzy . . .

Oops . . .

So I grabbed a servant's shoulders, and the soup bowl he was holding flew into the air . . .

must have upset his balance," she explained.

Trap muttered to me, "Sometimes it seems like your balance has been off since birth!"

"It is I who must excuse myself," de' Mousati said kindly. "Your brother has been reduced to this miserable state because of a brick that fell from my palazzo. I beg you to consider yourselves my guests for as long as you are here in Florence."

Then he clapped his paws, and two servants cleaned the room and brought me a new *embroidered coat*.

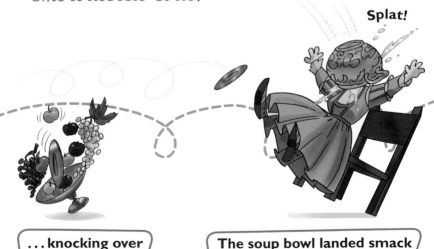

Splat!

... knocking over a bowl of fruit!

The soup bowl landed smack on a noblemouse's snout!

The rest of the evening continued without **incident**. Well, almost.

An hour later, a servant entered with a letter for Mousato de' Mousati. As he read it, an anxious look crossed his snout.

I happened to glance at the rodent sitting across from me. He was smirking. **How strange!**

This other rodent's name was WHISKELLO DE' WHISKERLIS. He had icy-gray eyes, a short little beard, and long, curled whiskers. There was something sinister about him. His

smile was **cold** — more of a grimace than a grin.

Dulcetta seemed concerned about her father, but she tried to liven up the conversation. "There's unrest in the city," she told us. "All these debates about whether **PAINTING** or ꜱꜰᴜꜱᴘᴛᴜꜰᴇ is the more noble art . . . and if the best artist is LEONARDO DA VINCI or *Michelangelo Buonarroti*!"

"It would be **fabumouse** to meet them," I said.

"Oh, of course that can be arranged!" Dulcetta replied. "Tomorrow I shall escort you to the place where Leonardo tries out his inventions."

I thanked her **happily**. Trap, on the other paw, immediately began boasting.

"Tomorrow two of the greeeaaat **mice of science** will meet: Leonardo da Vinci and Trap St . . . er, Trapolindo de' Stiltonini — that is, me!"

Dulcetta turned to me. "And you, Geronimuccio, what do you do?"

"My cousin works in **books**," Trap replied before I could get a squeak in edgewise.

"Really? If you are interested in the art of **printing**, there are shops here that use the new systems invented by **Gutenberg**,"* Dulcetta replied.

Suddenly, Mousato jumped to his paws. "This letter has brought me **terrible news**. My ship was anchored down at Arno River, but there was a fire, and now it has sunk!"

Whiskello didn't bat a whisker. It was almost as if he'd expected this news.

Strange! Very strange!

"Oh, your ship sank?" he said snidely. "Now I suppose you won't be able to repay your debt to me."

Mousato **sighed**. "That's right, I cannot pay the debt right now. Whiskello, could you give me more time? Otherwise I'm **ruined**!"

* See p. 195. Johannes Gutenberg (circa 1400–1468) created the first printing press that used movable type.

AN ANCIENT ART

For the rest of the evening, Dulcetta seemed worried. I saw her eyes fill with tears. But she gathered her strength. Before wishing us good night, she suggested we visit the workshop of the famouse printer MINO TIMPAGINO. I thanked her and promised I would definitely go tomorrow.

The next morning, we awoke very early. We left Mousato's palace and headed to the PONTE VECCHIO, Florence's famous "old bridge." Along the streets, the shops were opening their shutters for business.

"That's funny!" Bugsy observed. "There are only DYE shops on this street, and only carpenters on the next. And down there, there are only SHOEMAKERS, and on that one only Fabric stores . . ."

Thea smiled. "Yes, that was the custom back in the Renaissance. Rodents who practiced the same trade came together to form **corporations** — associations that helped fellow tradesmice and made common business rules. That's why they often opened **SHOPS** on the same street — it was easier to assist one another."

But I wasn't listening to them. I had noticed a familiar smell in the air . . . the smell of **PAPER**!

I FOLLOWED THE SCENT AS IF I WERE HYPNOTIZED . . .

. . . and ended up **smacking** my snout into two rodents transporting an enormouse load of paper!

Holey cheese, it was the two nosy rodents from the day before! **WHAT BAD LUCK!**

"Oh, it's you, *grullo*! What are you doing? You're ruining our paper!" they scolded me.

"Oh, it's the mice we met yesterday," I said.

"Beat it! You're just getting under paw here.

WE ARE WORKING," the rodents told me.

Trap **yanked** my ear. "Why can't you act normal just this once, Cousinkins?"

I ignored him. I was too busy caressing a precious sheet of vegetable paper. It was made from **cotton**. You see, I know a lot about paper. That's why I was so curious to see what was used back in the Renaissance.

Embarrassed, Thea dragged me away. "Please pardon my brother, he's always getting his paws in a pickle!"

A few steps later, we turned down a small street.

Huh?!

Oh, what magnificent paper . . .

There we spotted an **old-fashioned printing press**.

It was Mino Timpagino's press. He was the first master printer in Florence. (Or at least that's what it said on the **SIGN** outside his shop.)

I stopped in to visit. "Good day! May I squeak with you?"

A **big**, **bulky** rodent with paws like cheese wheels came to meet me. "Of course, sir. How may I help you?"

"I would like to visit your shop," I said. "I **love** books."

"You are interested in books? Then you will like my **machines** — they are the latest technology," he squeaked proudly. "They come from Germany. Just think, I can print **THREE**

or maybe even **FOUR BOOKS** a day!"

I scampered into the print shop and saw the shop mice bent over the printers. Some were holding movable letters, others were mixing the **INK**, and others still were **SEWING** the books' spines.

In one corner, a few rodents were making a hand press work. Curious, I went to get a better look. But at that moment, a shop mouse from the workshop dropped a **WOODEN CUBE** on the ground.

It was a small printing letter. I remember quite well that it was the letter **B**, as in **B**lockhead!

1. I knelt down to pick it up . . .

Here it is!

2. But my poor tail got **crushed** in the press. **YEE-OUCH!**

3. I **JUMPED** all over the room, stroking the tip of my tail . . . and hit the case of printing letters, which **flew** all over the place!

4. As I tried to pick them up, I accidentally put my 🐾🐾🐾 in the ink jar, spilling it all over the workshop. **CRUSTY KITTY LITTER, WHAT A CALAMITY!**

"What are you doing, signor?" Mino Timpagino yelled. "You've got a real talent for trouble, don't you! Clean up this **mess**, or you'll regret it!"

I spent the rest of the day scouring the workshop, putting all the papers in O R D E R, and reprinting the ruined pages — all under the watch of a scowling MINO TIMPAGINO.

In the end I was exhausted but happy. You see, over the course of the day, I had learned everything there was to know about the ancient art of PRINTING!

It was evening by the time I dragged my tail all the way to *Mousato de' Mousati's* palazzo. I was so tired, I went to bed without dinner.

I'm exhausted!

RODENT'S HONOR!

The next morning, *Dulcetta* woke us at dawn. Her fur was **VERY PALE** and her eyes were rimmed with RED, as if she'd been crying.

"What's wrong?" I asked her.

"My father was ~~ARRESTED~~ last night!" Dulcetta said.

"What? How is that possible?" Thea asked.

"To pay for his last shipment of goods from the East, my father borrowed many, many golden florins from Whiskello de' Whiskerlis, the crooked banker you met." Dulcetta sobbed. "Father had a week to pay him back, otherwise he would take our house and all our land. But since the ship sank, he can't pay. Last night I **begged** Whiskello to give us more time, but

he just laughed at me. Then he had my father arrested, and now my dear papa is in prison because of the **DEBT**!"

I was **madder** than a mouse in a trap. What a greedy, deceitful rodent! Poor Dulcetta, and poor Mousato!

We all gathered around to **console** her.

"You are not alone, Dulcetta. You can count on us! What can we do to help?" asked Thea, hugging her.

Dulcetta wiped away her **TEARS**. "Thank you!

We will help you!

You are true friends. But I don't know how you can help. The ship has already sunk! The only thing that can help Papa now is lots and lots of GOLD to pay his debt."

"Dulcetta, we'll find a way to help you pay the debt," I declared.

"WE WILL HELP, RODENT'S HONOR!"

we all squeaked together.

Dulcetta scurried away, and the rest of us sat down to figure out how we could find the money to help her and her father.

After an hour of racking our brains, Thea suggested **going out** to clear our snouts. We went toward **Mount Ceceri**, a hill outside Florence.

It was a splendid sunny morning. The **sky** was clear, and the wind ruffled our fur. The countryside was bright and green, and the birds were singing. But there was **sadness** in our hearts.

I was concentrating so hard on Dulcetta's problems that I didn't notice the time passing. Before I knew it, we'd reached **Mount Ceceri**.

Benjamin glanced up. "Uncle G, look at that **STRANGE BIRD**!" he cried. "Why does it keep running **UP** and **Down**?"

We followed his gaze, and then headed to the mountaintop to investigate. There we saw a chubby rodent racing back and forth. He had huge **WINGS** made of **WOOD** and **Fabric** tied to his shoulders. He was jumping up and down like a big chicken trying to take to the sky.

Near him, a distinguished, middle-aged rodent was taking notes in a *notebook*. I recognized  him at once. It was the genius LEONARDO DA VINCI, in the fur!

MORE OF A TURKEY THAN A FALCON . . .

Leonardo squeaked confidently to his helper. "**Zoroastro**,* are you ready to fly?"

Zoroastro peeked over the edge of the cliff. "Umm, Maestro, are you sure this will work?"

"Of course, Zoroastro. And if it doesn't, we'll make a new pair of wings," Leonardo said. "Come on, jump! Take flight as *gracefully as a nightingale, as powerfully as a pelican, as freely as a falcon . . .*"

"He seems much more like a **turkey** than a falcon," Trap muttered.

Zoroastro looked down. His snout was REALLY PALE.

---

* Master Tommaso Masini, known as Zoroastro, was da Vinci's assistant for many of his experiments.

"Don't you have any faith in science?" Leonardo demanded.

Trap interrupted them. "Hello, my name is Trapolindo de' Stiltonini, and I am a **scientist**, too. These are my friends Thea, Bugsina, Benjamino, and Geronimuccio."

Leonardo bowed. "Noblemice, welcome. You are about to witness an extraordinary flying experiment!"

"Fabumouse! But, Leo, this device will never work," Trap squeaked. "It's too heavy! You need plastic, nylon, and STEEL tubes, not wood and fabric."

Leonardo was insulted. "How dare you? My device will work perfectly!" he shouted, gnashing his whiskers.

Zoroastro quickly took Trap's side. "Maestro, even this gentlemouse says it won't work. I'm taking off the wings." He took a step back, but

he **TRIPPED** over his own tail! He rolled along the slope, shrieking as he **plummeted** downward.

We all watched in horror as he fell. "He's flying, all right. Like a penguin stuffed with Parmesan!" Trap muttered.

"Flap your wings, Zoroastro!" Leonardo called after him.

Zoroastro flapped his wings, but it didn't do any good. There was a small cloud of dust and a loud sound:

THUNK!

We were worried for Zoroastro, but then we saw him get up. "Ohh, that **hurt**!"

"Go get a **stretcher**!" Leonardo ordered his two other assistants. Then he turned to Trap. "Now, what were you saying before, foreigner? **PLASTIC?** What's that? **Nylon?** And where can I find **STEEL**?"

"Never mind," Trap replied. "You can't find this stuff anywhere in the Renaissance. But one day, everyone will be able to **fly**!"

Leonardo stared at Trap. "I like your **ideas**, sir. Would you want to collaborate with me?"

Trap shook his snout. "No, thanks, Leo. I'm just **TRAVELING** through!"

"I can pay you," Leonardo pleaded. "A nice sack of **gold florins**."

We exchanged glances. That money could help Dulcetta! So Trap told Leonardo, "Well, actually . . . I **WILL** share some of my scientific brilliance!"

"Thank you, kind sir," said Leonardo. He led us back to his workshop. There was an easel with a wooden plank, plaster SCULPTURES, models of machinery, and many DRAWINGS. I was more excited than a hungry rat in a cheese shop.

As Leonardo passed in front of the wooden PLANK, he sighed. "I don't know what to paint on this. What do you say, foreigner? Any ideas?"

"Do you know Leonardo's most famouse painting, the *Mona Mousa*?" I whispered to Trap.

Trap nodded. "Why, yes, Leo, I have the perfect idea for you! Take a famouse lady — say, the Mona Mousa of Giocondo — create a detailed portrait, showing her with a mysterious expression, where you can't tell if she's laughing or not. And you'll have a mouseterpiece!"

Leonardo stroked his whiskers. "I like it! I will start painting right away . . . and I'll call it *Mona Mousa*."

YOU LOOK LIKE A GIANT OCTOPUS!

Next, Leonardo showed us a strange leather **diving** suit, complete with a hood and two tubes emerging from a helmet. "Now, Sir Trapolindo, what do you think of this INVENTION? I haven't been able to test it yet. Will it work?"

Trap scratched his snout. "Hmm. Maybe yes, maybe no . . . but there's only **ONE WAY** to find out. Let's test it now! My cousin would be happy to try it out for us. Come on, Geronimo, put on the suit!"

"Don't even think about it!" I protested. "Leonardo just said he doesn't know if it works."

"Enough blathering, Gerrykins. Put on the suit! **You are standing in the way of science.**"

"Think of *Dulcetta*," Thea whispered to me.

"We need to earn that bag of gold florins."

Only then did I agree. After all, **I had promised to help her**!

Leonardo and Trap decided that we would test the invention in the **Arno River**.

When we reached the port, Thea turned to me. "Dulcetta told me her father's **BOAT** was anchored down there at that dock. Now it's underwater. Look, you can still see the tip of the mast poking above the surface!"

Will it work?

Put on the suit!

Don't even think about it!

That gave me an idea. I would take advantage of the fact that I was *underwater* to examine the ship. Maybe I'd be able to figure out why it **sank**.

I put on the suit, and Trap immediately began snickering. "You look like a *giant octopus!*"

There was no time to retort, because Trap latched the helmet over my snout and pushed me into the river!

The water was freezing . . . **Brrr!** Soon I had sunk to the muddy river bottom. I began to flail about in fear. I felt trapped like a MUMMY in a sarcophagus. I was as scared as a fish in a net!

I tried to calm down. I filled

my lungs with air. That's when I realized I could **breathe**! The diving suit worked.

I began to walk along the **BOTTOM** of the river. As soon as the mud settled, I saw I was close to the sunken ship.

Curiously, I began to examine it. There was a deep **GASH** in the hull, almost as if someone had destroyed the wood with an ax.

Oh my goodmouse, that's what had happened! Mousato's ship didn't sink because of a fire — someone had intentionally **damaged** it!

Satisfied with what I'd learned, I tugged the **ROPE** tied to my paw, and my **friends** pulled me up.

When I finally splashed out of the river, there was a little **EMERGENCY**. I absolutely had to go to the bathroom! I'd been stuck in that suit for a long time.

Leonardo solemnly thanked me for my help.

"Signor, because of you I was able to experiment with a new inven —"

I cut him short. "That's kind of you, but now I have to go to the **BATHROOM**."

Leonardo began to release the bolts, but then he shook his snout.

"ALAS, THE HELMET IS STUCK!"

Oh no! "Please help! This is **URGENT**!"

"Let me handle this," Trap **SHOUTED**. He grabbed the helmet and turned it to the **right**, then to the **left**. He'd almost unscrewed my snout from my neck, but the helmet still wouldn't come unstuck.

I began to **WEEP** in desperation.

Thank goodmouse for my sister. She took out a pair of **SCISSORS** and cut the suit. I was free!

SOMEONE? BUT WHO?

When I'd recovered, I had big news for my friends. "I've **discovered** something important. Mousato's ship did not sink because of a fire. Someone smashed a hole in the hull! The **FIRE** was a diversion."

"**SOMEONE? BUT WHO?**" Trap cried.

"Someone who wanted to harm Dulcetta's father," Thea said thoughtfully.

Benjamin nodded. "Someone like Whiskello!"

"You're right, Benjamin," I exclaimed. "**WHISKELLO** had plenty to gain by sinking the ship. He would get to take all of Mousato's property!"

Leonardo was happy with the help we'd given him. He went to get the sack of **florins** he'd promised us. But there was no time to wait — we absolutely had to find Dulcetta!

We *HURRIED* off. We found Dulcetta back in the palazzo, sniffling into her pawkerchief.

Thea and Bugsy scurried to her side and told her about what I'd discovered in the Arno.

Dulcetta **smiled** at me gratefully. "That wicked rat hoped no one would learn the truth! Thanks to you, my father and I are saved! I'm sure Whiskello never imagined that a courageous mouse like Geronimuccio would go to the bottom

I'm free! Hooray!

of the Arno to find proof of his **EVIL DEEDS**!"

We scurried to the Florentine **authorities** and asked to squeak with the magistrate Piero Soderini. When we told him that Whiskello had **sunk** the ship, he investigated.

Soon he released Dulcetta's father, and then he sent a group of soldiers to **ARREST** Whiskello and put him in prison instead, for fraud.

Mousato and Dulcetta **hugged** each other happily.

"Papa!"

"Dulcetta, my dear!"

"Our new friends were the ones who saved you," Dulcetta told her father. "They uncovered Whiskello's **SCAM**!"

Mousato thanked us. "Thanks to you, I am once again a free mouse!" Then he sighed. "Although my ship is still sunk and I don't have the **GOODS** I need for my business . . ."

Just then, Leonardo burst in, carrying a sack of florins. "Sir, here is your **gold**."

Trap's eyes sparkled. "**Excellent!** I'll take care of those, Leo!" he squeaked.

He was about to put the florins in his **BAG** when I cleared my squeak. "My friends, I believe Dulcetta and her father need this gold more than we do. They can use it to buy a new ship and restart their business!"

Trap glared at me. But he knew I was right. With a **heavy heart**, he pawed the gold over to

Mousato. "Okay, if I must . . ."

Fortunately, Leonardo had something that distracted my greedy cousin. It was his **PAINTING**! "What do you think, signor?" he asked.

Trap *sighed*. "The smile is all wrong . . . it needs to be more mysterious!" With a few quick brushstrokes, he changed the Mona Mousa's *smile*. "There, like that."

Before

"Signor Trapolindo, you are truly a prodigy!" Leonardo exclaimed.

"You see? Leo here says that I'm a *genius*!" Trap bragged.

As he babbled on, we said good-bye and returned

After

to the alley where the **PAW PRO PORTAL** was hidden. We'd had enough of an adventure in the Renaissance!

This time, we could leave calmly. For once, there was no one *CHASING* us! We had time to change out of our Renaissance outfits and into our modern-day clothes.

Our journey had ended. We were sad that our adventures were over, but it was nice to think that we were going back ***home*** . . .

Home. That word sounded so sweet. I calmly pressed the fourth **button** — the yellow one that would take us to New Mouse City.

This time, everything **SEEMED** to go well . . .

Everything **SEEMED** to work perfectly!

The portal began to buzz. We linked paws as we entered.

"New Mouse City, here we come!"

*New Mouse City . . .
at last!*

FINALLY HOME . . . OR NOT?!

As we entered the Paw Pro Portal, I felt like I was jumping into JELLY. Inside, the air was as dense as **FONDUE**, and though the feeling wasn't unpleasant, I couldn't wait to get out of there.

As we floated in the NOTHINGNESS, I saw images from the PAST and the FUTURE — plus infinite places on **EARTH** that I had never seen before.

Then I felt my head stop spinning. I ran out of the Paw Pro Portal and fell to my knees, kissïng the ground. "We're finally home!" I squeaked happily.

"Umm . . . you might not want to say that just yet, Uncle G!" said Bugsy Wugsy.

"Huh? Wh-what? Why?!" I cried, looking around.

It was **sunset**. All around us there was endless steppe, with low **dunes** rolling as far as the eye could see. The ground was **dirt** mixed with sand and covered with short thorny shrubs.

WHAT A DESOLATE PLACE!

Meanwhile, a freezing wind picked up and whistled **wildly**. It made my whiskers waver and my clothes twist.

I raised my squeak so my friends could hear me. "We **aren't** in New Mouse City! We **aren't** even on Mouse Island! We **aren't** home after all!" I **SHOUTED** in anguish.

I looked around more carefully. It really seemed as if we had ended up in a steppe area typical of **CENTRAL ASIA** . . . but in what period of history? It was impossible to tell. There were no buildings around and no one to ask for information.

Benjamin and Bugsy examined the **PAW PRO PORTAL**, skimming their paws over the buttons. Then they gave us some **TERRIBLE** news. "The control panel is stuck. It must have happened when Trap smacked the buttons back in ancient Greece."

"Rat-munching rattlesnakes, why do you always make stuff sound like my fault?" Trap **muttered**. "This is all Geronimo's fault! He made a mess of the **buttons**, playing with them like they were a video game . . ."

"That's enough *bickering*!" Thea scolded us. "First, let's try going back through the portal, and Geronimo can press the button for **home** again. Maybe it'll work this time."

"This time I want to press the button! Maybe I can manage to make it work," Trap said. "I know what I'm doing when it comes to **video games**, you know."

Hmpf!

It looks like a steppe . . .

I sighed. "It's not a video game, Trap. But if you want, you can press the button."

I headed toward the portal, but then I **STUMBLED**. At first I thought I was just tripping over my own tail, as usual. But then I realized the ground was trembling!

I looked up and saw a dense **cloud** of dust on the horizon. It was heading straight for us!

I squinted. A line of horses was galloping our way. On each horse there was a knight dressed in ruffled leather with a pointy helmet on his snout. The warriors had long WHiSKeRS that pointed downward. They were carrying swords that caught the fading rays of the sun.

As they drew closer, I could see a **warrior** leading the charge. He seemed very determined. Next to him there was a female rodent wearing FUR from a white steppe wolf.

They reminded me of a picture I'd seen in a

HISTORY book . . . but a book about what era?

Trap put his paw in front of his **EYES**. "Who in the name of string cheese could they be?"

Finally, it hit me. "Th-that's G-Genghis K-K-Kh . . ." I stuttered.

Trap turned to me. "Genghis who?"

I caught my breath and **YELLED** at the top of my lungs. "*GENGHIS KHAN!* One of the most feared conquerors of all time! The leader of the largest empire in all of history! And behind him is Börte, his beautiful and *daring* wife!"

GENGHIS KHAN
(CIRCA 1162–1227)

One of the most famous conquerors in history. This legendary warrior united the Mongol tribes, founded the Mongolian Empire, and led his troops to conquer a huge area, from the Pacific coast of Asia to the Adriatic Sea.

Trap *DARTED* toward the Paw Pro Portal. "Okay, so what are you waiting for? Move those paws! Let's ruuuuun!"

He leaped into the portal, **SHOUTING**, "I've had a change of heart, Gerrykins! Why don't you come in last and press the button? It's no cheese off my rind to **G⚙ FIRST**. See you in New Mouse City!"

I rolled my eyes. "Okay, come on, everyone! Get in the portal, quick! I'll try to make the buttons work so we can go home!"

When Thea, Trap, Bugsy, and Benjamin were safe inside, I tried to press the yellow button. But nothing happened: The portal didn't move.

My heart was in my snout. I tried again. The Mongols were getting closer and closer! I could hear the wind carrying their wild cries. Their shrill squeaks sent a chill down my tail.

I pressed the button again and again, more and more frantically. By now the Mongols were really close — so close I could see the magnetic look in GENGHIS KHAN'S eyes and the pearls in Börte's long fur . . .

"CAPTURE THAT RODENT!" Genghis Khan shouted to his followers.

Börte leaned off her horse. She was going to grab me by the tail!

At the last second, the portal **vibrated**, and I heard a familiar buzzing. Finally, the machine was working again!

I jumped into the portal just in time!

I saw the disappointment in Börte's eyes, but Genghis Khan just laughed.

Well done!

"Well done, friend! You're the first to say you escaped **GENGHIS KHAN**! But perhaps one day we will see each other again . . ."

Then he **winked** at me.

His grin was the last thing I saw before I **FELL** beyond the borders of space and time . . .

THE SMELL OF STEW AND THE SOUND OF A VIOLIN

I felt like I was diving into CLEAR jelly!

In the tunnel, the air was warm and thick like melted mozzarella . . .

My heart began to beat harder and harder . . .

MY EARS BUZZED . . .

My snout began to spin faster and faster, like I was stuck inside a blender. But the portal still wasn't working properly. The buzzing kept fading in and out, and the tunnel seemed much narrower.

When the buzzing and the vibrations ended, the portal stopped, but it leaned heavily to the left.

I rolled out first, since I was the last to enter.

Then my friends all **TUMBLED** out on top of me.

I got up with a groan. As soon as my snout cleared and I could **FOCUS**, I realized we were on the deck of a ship, and it was night.

Help!

Far away, in the darkness, I saw a light shining. It had to be the lighthouse in New Mouse City's port! TEARS came to my eyes at the thought of being home.

"Friends, we're back home!" I YELLED. From inside the ship, there was a lovely smell of cheese stew, and I could hear the sweet notes of a violin.

I sighed dreamily. "Food and music! We must be on a cruise ship ENTERING the port."

"What do you mean, romantic?" THEA replied. "Can't you tell what kind of ship this is?"

I strained my ears and realized someone was singing along with the music. I couldn't hear it well, because of the sound of the sea, but I heard strange words like treasure . . . and then BATTLE AT SEA and then black flag . . . and then SKULL . . .

"Skull? What skull?" I squeaked in alarm.

I lifted my gaze and saw a black flag blowing

in the breeze above our snouts!

I was about to let out a scream of fright, but Bugsy covered my mouth.

"Uncle G, do you want them to find us?"

A chill slid down my tail.

"Rancid rat hairs! W-we e-ended up on a p-p-pirate ship?!"

Trap scurried toward us — he had gone to look around. "Bad news, ratlings. The PIRATES are ugly, evil, and there are a lot of them! They are also armed up to their whiskers."

At that moment, a gruff squeak close to us shouted, "Sailor, portside! Lift the foresail and HAUL DOWN the fore topgallant . . ."

"Hoist the mainsail!" another cried.

Then a chorus of squeaks rose up around us.

They sounded **ghastlier** than a ghosts as they sang:

"We are many, pirates we be.
Up to our whiskers we're stocked with weaponry!
Yes, we be pirates, the ferocious herd
Of the one and only Captain Blackbeard!"

I **shuddered**. "I know who he is! He struck fear into the fur of rodents everywhere! His real name is Edward Teach, but everyone calls him **BLACKBEARD**."

EDWARD TEACH
BETTER KNOWN AS
BLACKBEARD
(CIRCA 1680–1718)
A famous British pirate and the terror of the Virginia and Carolina coastlines and the Caribbean Sea from 1716–1718.

Eek!

Eek!

Eek!

Eek!

A voice behind us thundered, *"Beware, for I am Blackbeard!*

"**B** as in '**B**eware of my ship, you dirty spies!'

L as in '**L**ifeboats won't help you now!'

A as in '**A**nd now you'll regret coming onboard my ship!'

C as in '**C**ome closer so I can make you walk the plank!'

K as in '**K**now that you're about to receive the lesson of a lifetime!'

B as in '**B**ehind **BARS** is where you'll end up — if you're lucky!'

E as in '**E**scape will be impossible!'

A as in '**A**nd the more I think about it, perhaps I should just feed you to the SHARKS.'

R as in '**R**ethinking things, maybe I'll just tie your tails to the flagpole!'

D as in '**D**efinitely . . . that's what I'll do!'"

"Quick, let's haul tail!" Thea **SHRIEKED**. "If we want to keep our tails, that is!"

We jumped to our paws, but Blackbeard just laughed. "**Ha, ha, ha!** Escaping? Ridicumouse! Where do you think you'll go, you lousy landlubbers? You are in the middle of the **sea**. Unless you grow **WINGS** like a seagull, you're in trouble, or my name isn't Blackbeard!"

But we were already running to the **PAW PRO PORTAL**, and I was pressing the button to take us home, hoping desperately that it would work.

It did, immediately. **THANK GOODMOUSE!**

Thwack! Blackbeard's sword grazed the tip of my tail as I dove into the portal.

A **buzz**, a **tremor** . . . and once again we were traveling through space and time . . .

A LEGENDARY LOCOMOTIVE

After the usual whirlwind, the **PAW PRO PORTAL** let us out onto something made of metal. It seemed to have two narrow bars with wooden ties and really large **BOLTS**. Then I heard a train whistle in the distance.

"We're on train tracks! **HOORAY!** We are finally in the present — we are home!" I cried.

"Geronimo, as usual, you can't see the holes for the cheese!" Thea cried. "We've come to a *time* when there are **TRAINS**, but that doesn't mean we're home!"

"Look at how these rodents are dressed!" Trap squeaked. "Does this seem like New Mouse City in the twenty-first century to you?"

I **LOOKED** up. Surrounding us was a crowd

of rodents wearing old-fashioned suits, long dresses, and hats. Maybe it was a costume party? Or the set of a period m**o**vi**e**? Or . . . alas, my friends were probably right. We were still in the past!

Suddenly, all the rodents began to wave their paws frantically. Then I heard a really loud whistle, and I saw a cloud of gray smoke at the end of the tracks.

It was a long, narrow locomotive with **WOODEN** and metal wheels, with a tall smokestack letting out puffs of steam.

The train let out another whistle. That's when I realized it was speeding toward us!

"B-but that is the *Rocket*, the legendary locomotive DESIGNED by George Stephenson!" I stammered.

"It might be legendary,

Whaaat?

but if it **CRUSHES** us, we'll all be mouse meatballs!" Trap squeaked.

Trap jumped back into the portal, and Benjamin, Bugsy, and Thea followed him.

The locomotive let out a third whistle and the train driver poked his snout out the window. "Move off the tracks or you'll be squashed!"

But I couldn't: The Paw Pro Portal was right next to the tracks, and it didn't want to budge! There was no way I could press the **button** if I moved off the tracks.

Panicking, I kept pressing the home button. At last I heard a buzz . . .

Finally!

A moment before the *Rocket* ran over me, I leaped into the portal. I will never forget the stunned **EXPRESSION** on the driver's snout!

A moment later, we were **suspended** in time and space. We floated in absolute darkness . . .

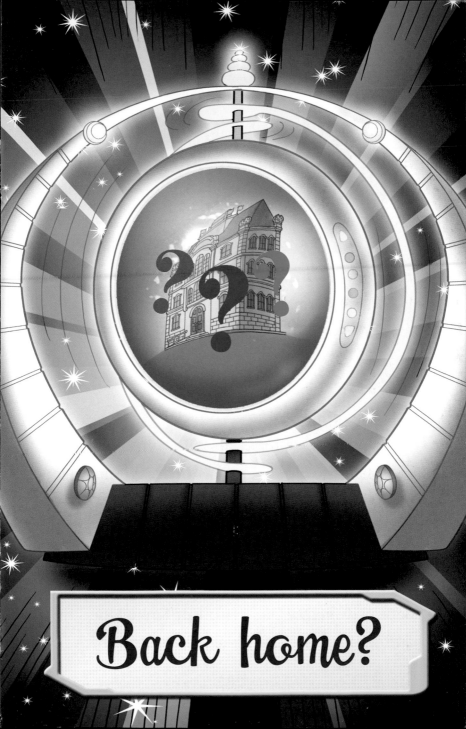

Back home?

FINALLY HOME . . .
FOR REAL THIS TIME!

I looked around frantically. **Where were we?**
Had we actually returned home? I couldn't figure
it out. We were in complete **darkness**!

Finally, we heard a familiar squeak.

"Friends, welcome home!"

It was Professor von Volt! This time, we had
really returned to Mouse Island.

I heard the click of a **SWITCH**, and light
flooded the laboratory. Professor von Volt's
friendly snout appeared, and he scurried up
to us eagerly. "How was your **TRIP**? Were
you able to study the mammoths? Did you visit
ancient Greece? Did you meet any of the great
Renaissance masters, like Leonardo da Vinci?"

"Yes. And modestly squeaking, I taught him a few things. Without us, he could hardly get a thing done," **Trap** bragged. "Leo is a good ratlet, but a bit limited. Luckily, he met a genius like me!"

Thea put a paw over his snout. "That's enough, Cousin. The professor has a lot of questions to ask us, and we have a lot to tell him!"

WE SPENT HOURS AND HOURS TELLING PROFESSOR VON VOLT ABOUT ALL OF OUR TIME-TRAVELING EXPERIENCES!

His eyes sparkled with excitement. As we squeaked, he tapped away at his **computer**, making notes about anything and everything.

The professor was very pleased with what we'd

learned, although he felt terrible about the buttons getting **STUCK**. He promised he'd keep working on the **PAW PRO PORTAL** till it was perfect.

"Next time, the portal will be even better. You'll see!" he said.

Then he shot us a worried look. "There will be a next time, right? You would like to go on another adventure to visit other historical times, right?"

"Of course! We would be HONORED to go on another trip!" Thea reassured him.

Benjamin nodded. "These trips are really mouserific! I still can't believe we spent a few days with the mammoths in the ICE AGE! We just studied that era of history in school with Miss Angel Paws . . . and I got to see it in person!"

Before I could reply, I heard a noise that sounded like a gurgle: GlugG!

Trap snickered and rubbed his belly. "Before we

leave on our next journey through time, I need to eat.

I'M PREHISTORICALLY HUNGRY!

And is that the lovely scent of **cheese**, or is my snout playing tricks on me again?"

The professor smiled and took us to another room, where a huge banquet awaited us.

"Well, I don't have a mammoth in the refrigerator, but I did prepare some cheese

Yum!

puffs, a TRIPLE-MOZZARELLA pizza, a few Cheesy Chews, a nice pot of fondue, a sweet cheese pie, some pear and Swiss smoothies, and . . ."

I didn't hear anything else he said. I was too busy stuffing my snout.

After the banquet, we came out of Professor von Volt's **underground** laboratory.

The first shadows of evening were falling on Mouse Island. Soon we would be in **New Mouse City** . . .

Ah, sweet **New Mouse City** . . . the place where every mouse wants to live!

The place where I left my **heart** during our long, exciting journey!

It was nice to go on an adventure, and I was looking forward to our next one! But it was even nicer to COME BACK. Back to the most beautiful place in the world . . . back *home*!

TRAVEL JOURNAL

Dear mouse friends,

What a fabumouse journey! We experienced so many wild adventures together, my whiskers are still shaking with excitement!

To remember our journey through time, I prepared this travel journal for you, full of fun quizzes and activities. Enjoy!

Your friend,

Geronimo Stilton

BACK IN TIME TO . . .
THE ICE AGE

POP QUIZ

DO YOU KNOW ABOUT

1 **DURING THE PLEISTOCENE EPOCH, WHAT DID OUR ANCESTORS DO TO SURVIVE?**

   a) They spent their days lazing about their cave.
   b) They hunted and gathered berries and roots.
   c) They worked in manufacturing.

2 **WHAT DID THE NEANDERTHALS EAT?**

   a) Only vegetables — they were vegetarians!
   b) Only baked goods — they loved sweets.
   c) The meat that they hunted, or the fruit and wild roots they gathered.

3 **HOW DID THE NEANDERTHALS LIGHT FIRES?**

   a) With matches.
   b) They rubbed wood or stones together until they made a spark.
   c) They didn't know how to light a fire.

NEANDERTHAL LIFE?

❹ WHERE DID OUR ANCESTORS LIVE?

a) In caves and huts made of mammoth bones and covered in furs.

b) In skyscrapers more than a hundred stories tall.

c) On large farms with other families.

❺ HOW DID THE NEANDERTHALS DRESS?

a) In the fur and leather of the animals they hunted.

b) In practical clothes like jeans and sweatshirts. They loved to be comfortable!

c) They wore heavy armor.

❻ WHEN DID THE MAMMOTHS BECOME EXTINCT?

a) They aren't extinct. They still live in nature preserves.

b) A few decades ago.

c) Thousands of years ago.

Answers: 1-b; 2-c;
3-b, 4-a, 5-a, 6-c

MAKE A BEAR-TOOTH NECKLACE

YOU NEED:
- a package of modeling clay
- a toothpick
- white and yellow poster paint and a paintbrush
- brown leather string (about twenty inches long)

1. Using the clay, make a cone about one and a half inches tall. Then make six smaller cones (each about an inch long).

2. Round the tallest part of each cone with your fingers. Then slightly curve the edges to one side. The cones should look like large bear teeth.

3. Using a toothpick, make a hole in each "tooth." Make sure it's big enough for the string to fit through. Let the clay dry for a few days.

4 Prepare the paint in an old jar or plastic container. Add a bit of yellow to the white, and then paint the "bear teeth" and let them dry.

5 String the biggest "tooth" halfway down the string and tie knots on either side to hold it there. Then slip the other "teeth" onto the string, three on each side of the big tooth.

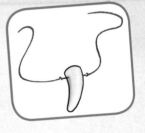

6 Tie the ends of the necklace together, making sure there is enough room for your head to fit through.

Your bear-tooth necklace is ready!

MAMMOTH BOOKMARK

YOU NEED: poster board, safety scissors, colored pencils or markers, and a glue stick

1 Make a photocopy of the mammoth on this page.

2 Glue it onto the poster board and color the mammoth with pencils or markers.

3 Cut your mammoth along the dotted lines.

4 Slip the page of your book between the tusks and the trunk. When you return to your book, the mammoth will show you the right page. Happy reading!

BACK IN TIME TO . . .

ANCIENT GREECE

POP QUIZ

DO YOU KNOW ABOUT

❶ IN ANCIENT GREECE, WHAT WAS THE AGORA?

a) A large mall with a multiroom movie theater.

b) The city's main square — the town's economic, commercial, and religious center.

c) A famous restaurant in Athens where Socrates and Plato would often go to discuss philosophy.

❷ WHO WAS SOCRATES?

a) A very famous Greek cook.

b) An ancient Greek philosopher.

c) The sculptor of the statue of Athena in the Parthenon.

❸ WHAT WAS THE SYMPOSIUM FOR THE ANCIENT GREEKS?

a) A banquet during which men would sing, dance, and play games.

b) A traditional couples' dance.

c) A type of Peloponnesian wine.

ANCIENT GREECE?

4 **WHAT WAS THE GREAT PANATHENAEA?**

a) An important festival dedicated to the goddess Athena.

b) What ancient Greeks called summer vacation.

c) A sporting event that took place in Olympia every four years.

5 **WHO WAS XANTHIPPE?**

a) A famous priestess of Athens.

b) Socrates's wife.

c) The goddess of justice.

6 **WHAT WAS THE PEPLOS?**

a) A fashionable ankle boot in ancient Greece.

b) A kind of bathing suit worn by women in ancient Greece.

c) A tunic made of the finest fabric, worn by women in ancient Greece.

Answers: 1-b, 2-b, 3-a, 4-a, 5-b, 6-c.

MAKE A COLUMN PIGGY BANK!

YOU NEED:

- a cardboard tube (a paper towel roll is perfect)
- poster board
- some corrugated cardboard, with lines on the inside
- white paint
- a glue stick
- safety scissors

1. Using the outside of your cardboard tube as a stencil, draw two circles on the poster board. Then add eight small rectangles to the edge of each circle.

2. Cut the first circle and use it to close the edge of one side of the tube. Glue the rectangles to the outside of the tube to keep it shut.

3. On the second circle, cut a rectangular opening in the middle so a large coin can fit through. Then close that end of the tube by gluing the circle's rectangles to the edges.

4) Now glue the lined, corrugated cardboard over the outside of the tube.

5) Cut a strip of the corrugated cardboard (with the lines going horizontally) as wide as the tube, but longer at each end by three inches.

6) Make a cut in the cardboard as long as the one you made on the second circle (see step 3).

7) Glue the cardboard to the top so that the two cuts line up. Then roll the edges toward the tube to form the top of the column. Use the picture on the right to help you.

8) Paint the column with white paint.

Now all you need to do is fill it with money!

AN OLYMPIC AFTERNOON

Throw a mini Olympic Games with friends!

YOU NEED: chalk, a Frisbee, a few cardboard tubes, a container (like a garbage can or bucket)

(1) For the **RACE**, draw a starting line and finish line on the ground with chalk. Ask an adult to start the race and name the winners.

(2) For the **DISCUS LAUNCH**, trace a circle on the ground. Stand inside the circle one by one to throw a Frisbee. Whoever's Frisbee goes the farthest wins!

(3) For the **RELAY RACE**, form teams of at least two players each. In addition to a starting line, draw some lines farther into the race course that are all the same distance apart for the other runners on each team to stand at. Put a container on the finish line to be the Olympic cauldron. The first runner to leave must carry a cardboard tube, and must pass it off to the next runner on their team, and so on. The team of the runner who finishes and lights the Olympic cauldron first (throws their tube in the container) wins!

BACK IN TIME TO . . .
THE RENAISSANCE

PØP QUIZ

DO YOU KNOW ABOUT

1 WHAT WAS THE MOST IMPORTANT INVENTION OF THE RENAISSANCE?

a) The movable type printing press.
b) The wheel.
c) Sparkling water.

2 DURING THE RENAISSANCE, THE BEST PAINTERS, SCULPTORS, AND ARTISANS . . .

a) Loved making graffiti in caves and caverns.
b) Were inspired by the art of the Neanderthals.
c) Had their own workshops where they taught their crafts to apprentices.

3 THE RENAISSANCE IS CONSIDERED THE BEGINNING OF:

a) The Dark Ages.
b) The modern age.
c) Deep-sea exploration.

THE RENAISSANCE?

❹ CORPORATIONS WERE:

a) Stores where people could buy clothes and other goods.
b) Soccer associations.
c) Powerful associations of artists, artisans, and merchants who established work rules.

❺ LEONARDO DA VINCI PAINTED:

a) A portrait of Geronimo Stilton.
b) The *Mona Lisa*.
c) The famous *Still Life with Pizza*.

❻ IN THE RENAISSANCE, WOMEN WORE:

a) Mostly pants.
b) One-piece suits made of mammoth fur.
c) A long crinkly skirt attached to a tight bodice with a square neckline and highly stylized sleeves.

LEONARDO'S PARACHUTE

Follow these instructions carefully!

1. To make two parachutes of different sizes, cut one 12 x 12-inch square out of the tissue paper and one square that's 8 x 8 inches.

2. With tape, attach to the four corners of each parachute strings that are each six inches long.

3 Knot the strings of the parachute together. Make sure the tape that is attached to the corners stays on the outside.

4 Attach two paper clips (or a piece of candy) to the strings of each parachute so that each one is carrying the same weight.

5 Make sure an adult is with you, and carefully stand on a chair to let your parachutes go. Which parachute moves faster? To help them float gently, you can make a hole in the middle of the parachutes — this will help the air flow more easily.

Are you ready to make your parachutes fly?

Leonardo's strange writing!

Leonardo's strange writing!

Leonardo used a secret writing system to write his notes. In fact, he was able to read easily both backward and forward.

Try reading this sentence:

GERONIMO STILTON'S JOURNEYS THROUGH TIME

···

If you can't decipher it, you can read it using a mirror ... the reflection will give you the answer!

Use Leonardo's writing to send coded messages or to write your secrets! You just need two sheets of thin paper. Write your message on one sheet, then flip it over. Put the other sheet of paper on top of it, holding the sheets up to a window if necessary, and trace the backward message onto the other sheet of paper. Remember ... if you don't want your message to be deciphered, don't leave MIRRORS lying around!

Be sure to read all my fabumouse adventures!

#1 Lost Treasure of the Emerald Eye

#2 The Curse of the Cheese Pyramid

#3 Cat and Mouse in a Haunted House

#4 I'm Too Fond of My Fur!

#5 Four Mice Deep in the Jungle

#6 Paws Off, Cheddarface!

#7 Red Pizzas for a Blue Count

#8 Attack of the Bandit Cats

#9 A Fabumouse Vacation for Geronimo

#10 All Because of a Cup of Coffee

#11 It's Halloween, You 'Fraidy Mouse!

#12 Merry Christmas, Geronimo!

#13 The Phantom of the Subway

#14 The Temple of the Ruby of Fire

#15 The Mona Mousa Code

#16 A Cheese-Colored Camper

#17 Watch Your Whiskers, Stilton!

#18 Shipwreck on the Pirate Islands

#19 My Name Is Stilton, Geronimo Stilton

#20 Surf's Up, Geronimo!

#21 The Wild, Wild West

#22 The Secret of Cacklefur Castle

A Christmas Tale

#23 Valentine's Day Disaster

#24 Field Trip to Niagara Falls

#25 The Search for Sunken Treasure

#26 The Mummy with No Name

#27 The Christmas Toy Factory

#28 Wedding Crasher

#29 Down and Out Down Under

#30 The Mouse Island Marathon

#31 The Mysterious Cheese Thief

Christmas Catastrophe

#32 Valley of the Giant Skeletons

#33 Geronimo and the Gold Medal Mystery

#34 Geronimo Stilton, Secret Agent

#35 A Very Merry Christmas

#36 Geronimo's Valentine

#37 The Race Across America

#38 A Fabumouse School Adventure

#39 Singing Sensation

#40 The Karate Mouse

#41 Mighty Mount Kilimanjaro

#42 The Peculiar Pumpkin Thief

#43 I'm Not a Supermouse!

#44 The Giant Diamond Robbery

#45 Save the White Whale!

#46 The Haunted Castle

#47 Run for the Hills, Geronimo!

#48 The Mystery in Venice

#49 The Way of the Samurai

#50 This Hotel Is Haunted!

#51 The Enormouse Pearl Heist

#52 Mouse in Space!

#53 Rumble in the Jungle

#54 Get into Gear, Stilton!

#55 The Golden Statue Plot

#56 Flight of the Red Bandit

Special Edition!

The Hunt for the Golden Book

#57 The Stinky Cheese Vacation

#58 The Super Chef Contest

#59 Welcome to Moldy Manor

Special Edition!

The Hunt for the Curious Cheese

#60 The Treasure of Easter Island

#61 Mouse House Hunter

#62 Mouse Overboard!

Special Edition!

The Hunt for the Secret Papyrus

#63 The Cheese Experiment

Be sure to read all my adventures in the Kingdom of Fantasy!

THE KINGDOM OF FANTASY

THE QUEST FOR PARADISE:
THE RETURN TO THE KINGDOM OF FANTASY

THE AMAZING VOYAGE:
THE THIRD ADVENTURE IN THE KINGDOM OF FANTASY

THE DRAGON PROPHECY:
THE FOURTH ADVENTURE IN THE KINGDOM OF FANTASY

THE VOLCANO OF FIRE:
THE FIFTH ADVENTURE IN THE KINGDOM OF FANTASY

THE SEARCH FOR TREASURE:
THE SIXTH ADVENTURE IN THE KINGDOM OF FANTASY

THE ENCHANTED CHARMS:
THE SEVENTH ADVENTURE IN THE KINGDOM OF FANTASY

THE PHOENIX OF DESTINY:
AN EPIC KINGDOM OF FANTASY ADVENTURE

THE HOUR OF MAGIC:
THE EIGHTH ADVENTURE IN THE KINGDOM OF FANTASY

And don't miss my first two journeys through time!

THE JOURNEY THROUGH TIME

BACK IN TIME:
THE SECOND JOURNEY THROUGH TIME